Disc 10-19-2016

WITHDRAWN

WHITE DESERT

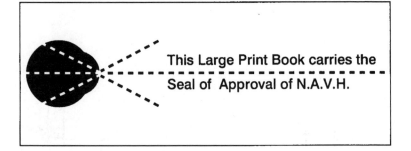

WHITE DESERT

Loren D. Estleman

Thorndike Press • Waterville, Maine

Published in 2002 by arrangement with St. Martin's Press, LLC.

Thorndike Press Large Print Western Series.

The tree indicium is a trademark of Thorndike Press.

The text of this Large Print edition is unabridged.
Other aspects of the book may vary from the original edition.

Cover design by Thorndike Press Staff.

Set in 16 pt. Plantin.

Printed in the United States on permanent paper.

Library of Congress Cataloging-in-Publication Data

Estleman, Loren D.
    White desert / Loren D. Estleman.
      p. cm.
    ISBN 0-7862-3854-2 (lg. print : hc : alk. paper)
    1. Canada, Northern — Fiction. 2. Large type books.
I. Title.
PS3555.S84 W48 2002
  813'.54—dc21   2001056507

For Barbara Puechner,
in her memory:
It's not a tragedy
that she left us so soon.
The miracle is
that we had her as long as we did.

PART ONE

Maintain the Right

.

1

Forty years have passed, and I still can't look at a game of billiards without thinking that's the game that got me shot in Canada. I don't mind telling you it's spoiled me for indoor sports.

In September 1881, Judge Harlan A. Blackthorne suffered a heart attack, the first totally selfish act I had known him to commit in his long tenure on the federal bench in Helena, Montana Territory. It happened while he was presiding over a case of rape and murder on the Blackfoot reservation. He was quiet in his habits, and his seizure was no exception; the opposing sides went on pleading their cases for several minutes until the prosecutor raised a point of law, and when Blackthorne didn't rule right away, the lawyers noticed his slumped posture and gray coloring and after arguing about it for another minute sent for a doctor.

The Judge spent the next six weeks in bed, during which Chester Arthur replaced him with a carpetbagger named Kennedy, whose legal instructions resulted in more hung juries than had ever taken place in the history of the territory. (Four years later Grover Cleveland named him assistant secretary of the treasury.) In November, a reluctant Dr. Albert Schachter allowed his heart patient to resume his duties, on the condition that he abandon his practice of studying the docket on Sunday and seek lighter recreation. Blackthorne gave his word that he would.

I should have known right then that trouble was making my bed.

To pledge one's word was never a light thing among frontiersmen, who knew that straying from it invited swift and bloody retribution. The Judge, who had no such fear, valued his honor as did few gentlemen born. (He was the son of a failed farmer and self-educated.) Anyone else in his position might have driven a couple of wooden stakes ninety feet apart in some town lot and started pitching horseshoes. Harlan A. Blackthorne, deciding that billiards were the thing, sent all the way to Chicago for the most expensive table and accessories featured in the Montgomery Ward catalogue. The shipment traveled by rail to the end of the line in western

Dakota, where it was loaded aboard a wagon and freighted four hundred miles overland to Helena. This took another six weeks, the last part of it during the first blizzard of January 1882; one horse died from exhaustion and Dr. Schachter treated two members of the crew for frostbite. But the table and its equipment arrived intact.

At the time the order was placed, Blackthorne was not entirely himself, or he would have known where to put the table when it came. Since he had not used federal funds to make the purchase, he was loath to take up space in the courthouse, and the only room that would have answered in his house outside town contained his wife's pump organ. This item would vacate the premises only in the company of Mrs. Blackthorne herself. At length he entered into an arrangement with Chink Sherman, manager of the Merchants Hotel: In return for allowing the table to occupy a guest room in the establishment, Sherman would have the use of the pump organ the first and third Saturday of every month to rehearse the Sacred Hearts of Jesus and Mary Choir, of which he was master. Mrs. Blackthorne, a Presbyterian and the daughter of a thirty-third-degree Freemason, was rewarded for her assent with the gift of a Jewel stove, to be shipped from Detroit sometime in the spring. Observers who amused themselves with arithmetical problems concluded that the Judge's heart attack had at this point set him back some eight hundred fifty dollars, not counting Schachter's fee.

The owner of the billiard table, however, was satisfied. The hotel was no more than a brisk, doctor-approved walk from both the courthouse and his home, refreshments were available from the Merchants' kitchen and bar, and he had a place to amuse himself when court was in recess. Not to mention the first and third Saturday of every month, when his house was invaded by tone-deaf Catholics.

It was a beautiful table, carved from Central American mahogany the color of oxblood, with mesh pockets and a green baize top as thick as the rugs in Chicago Joe's whorehouse. The slate alone weighed three hundred pounds and had required six men to carry inside. The cues were made of white ash, hand rubbed to a golden finish and straight, the balls of enameled African ivory. Nothing had been seen like it in town since Uncle Abe Cotton, one of the first prospectors to tap into the lode, fell ill of pneumonia and ordered a custom coffin all the way from San Francisco; and in fact the Judge's billiard set might have had the edge, although no one was willing to dig up Uncle Abe to make the comparison. Pierpont Morgan was said to have installed the same set in his Fifth Avenue mansion. There really was no reason, given the quality of the equipment and his frequent use of it, that Judge Blackthorne should have been the worst player west of New York and east of Hong Kong.

No man alive could get the better of the pioneer jurist in a battle of wills or wits. Reliable witnesses claimed to have heard him call Boss Tweed a crook to his face, at a time when a twitch of the Tweed eyebrow could have brought down the chief justice of the Supreme Court, and I was present in his courtroom the day he talked the defendant in a murder case out of the pistol he had snatched from the bailiff when none of the armed officers present dared risk a shot for fear of hitting the Judge. But the balls on that table were unimpressed by his reputation. He was incapable of making the simplest shot. Worse, he insisted upon attempting the most complicated banks, with results that ranged between pathetic and disastrous; a sternly worded letter from the State Department had been addressed to him after he bounced the four ball off the forehead of a visiting Russian grand duke. At that point the table had been in his possession three years, and he had been practicing almost daily. The game I'm talking about now took place three days after it arrived.

At that point he had played a couple of dozen games with deputy marshals and other employees of his court, most of whom had been hard put to lose to him. I should mention here that the American justice system never had a fairer man than when Blackthorne was on the bench. Although he hanged forty-seven men, a record for legal executions in the Northwest, a judicial review of those cases in 1901 found that the evidence presented would have held up in any proceedings in the country, and that in fact the Judge had in each case allowed the defense greater latitude than precedent required. Unfortunately, this balance did not always apply to his behavior once court was adjourned. He played favorites, stooped to nothing short of blackmail to work his will with associates and inferiors, and never forgave a humiliation, no matter how trivial. Most of all he hated to lose. He never ran out of ways to torture subordinates who forgot themselves and bested him in a game of skill.

I was the lone exception. I was a long way from his pet and would more than likely have hanged for his murder if I didn't spend most of my time hundreds of miles from the capital, chasing fugitives and transporting prisoners; a lifetime of sudden justice hadn't done much to develop my Christian understanding, and Blackthorne was as hard to get along with as a bad case of the shingles. However, there was no misery he could arrange for me that compared with what I faced most of the time I was doing my part to enforce the law in the territories. He must have sensed that early in our acquaintance, because after a couple of half-hearted attempts to make me plead for mercy he left off trying and contented himself with black looks and short-fused retorts whenever I managed to make him appear less than omnipotent.

Which wasn't that often, except in billiards. He was the best and smartest man I ever knew, as well as the pettiest and worst tempered.

He rose in darkness and was seldom up

after ten at night. This Sunday — the first since the table was delivered — was different. There were twenty inches of snow on the ground, a forty-mile-an-hour wind was whipping up twelve-foot drifts, and neither of us was in any hurry to wrap himself in his furs and go home until Montana decided to lie down for the night. His credit with Chink Sherman was good enough to swing us rooms in the hotel, but he wasn't about to do that. I had beaten him six games in succession; he was determined to win one before we packed it in. I was just as determined not to let him, tired as I was. That kind of thing can become a habit. The frontier was a forest of wooden markers bearing the names of deputy U.S. marshals who had decided to show someone mercy. None of them was going to read PAGE MURDOCK because I broke my own precedent with a stick in my hands.

Blackthorne shot first after the break. He was in his vest and shirtsleeves, rare event. Almost no one saw him that way except when he was changing out of his robes into his Prince Albert coat, but we were both working up a sweat in the overheated room. Leaning across the table under the light of the hanging Chesterfield lamp, the

Judge's hair and beard were as black as onyx and his lips were compressed into a Mona Lisa smirk of intense concentration. His teeth fit poorly, and he seldom wore them when he wasn't in court, but he was vain of his looks and didn't want to show his gums when he smiled.

"Bliss and Whitelaw are in Canada," he said, and shot. For once the ball went into the pocket.

"Wishful thinking?" I chalked my cue. His luck couldn't hold.

He shook his head. "I got a wire this morning from an Inspector Vivian with the North-West Mounted. The gang hit a settlement on the Saskatchewan over Christmas, wiped out the population, and rode away with everything that wasn't frozen to the ground. They weren't in such a hurry they forgot to set fire to the town. There's nothing left."

I watched him line up his next shot. "If they wiped out the population, who identified Bliss and Whitelaw?"

"That's what identified them." This one missed the pocket by six inches.

"Could have been Indians."

"The inspector doesn't think so. Their beef is with the railroad. Anyway, Indians haven't much use for gold."

I waited for the cue ball to roll to a stop and studied the choice. "How much gold?"

"A few hundred. The settlement was made up of panners and their wives. Nobody was scalped. There were some throats cut, and some of the women were naked, probably stripped and raped, but there were bullet holes in most of the corpses, what was left of them. Indians aren't that wasteful with their ammunition. Bliss and Whitelaw spend it like water."

"Stakes seem low." I made my choice and sank the shot. The cue ball bounced off a cushion and clicked against the eight.

"You're forgetting they destroyed a village in the Cherokee strip for less. Tricky shot."

I ignored him and pocketed the six. The eight tried to follow but ran out of momentum at the edge. I stopped holding my breath. "Bliss and Whitelaw it is," I said. "What makes it our problem and not the Mounties'?"

"Eight banks in Wyoming and Montana, a train in Colorado, and thirty or forty dead across four territories, including mine. I'm sending a deputy up to advise the redcoats. He'll supervise the extradition when they're caught."

I missed the next shot, a simple bank.

"Not me. I'm on holiday."

"Since when?"

The grandfather's clock in the lobby struck eleven. "Since eleven o'clock. You promised me a month off after I did you that favor in New Mexico Territory last year. I never took it."

He took his turn and missed. "Damn. What are you going to do with a month off in the middle of a Montana winter?"

"Eat steak, drink whiskey, and loaf. Beat you at billiards. Read *Ben Hur*. Run up my bill at Chicago Joe's. Cut a hole in the Missouri and hook bass. Take good care of the parts I'd just freeze off in Canada. The only reason anyone lives up there is Cornwallis lost." I chalked my cue more energetically than usual.

"I could order you to go."

"I could take off my badge."

"You never wear it."

"That's not the point."

He thumped the butt of his cue against the floor. "There's a friendly way of settling this."

I grinned. "What are you putting up?"

"Two months off," he said. "Starting anytime you say."

"This game, or do you want to start fresh?"

"This one will do. I believe it's your shot."

The game went back and forth twice and then I ran the table. At the end, the eight ball was in direct line with the corner pocket with the cue ball perched halfway between it and the opposite corner. A drunken Indian could have made it. I took my time and shot. The eight dropped in. The cue ball teetered on the edge and went right in after it. I threw down my stick with an oath my father used to use; he'd learned it from Jim Beckwourth.

"Scratch," Blackthorne said. "I'll wire Inspector Vivian to expect you."

2

What anyone in 1882 knew for sure about Lorenzo Bliss and Charlie Whitelaw didn't begin to stack up to the lore.

It hasn't gotten any better. Every year, it seems, someone publishes a new book about one or the other or both, and all it does is embroider upon the malarkey that appeared in every journal from the old Indian Nations to Dakota, and as far east as New York and Boston. If you took it all for gospel, you had to wonder why the authorities in four territories had so much trouble locating a pair of killers ten feet tall riding at the head of an army of a thousand men.

After four decades of dime novels, saloon ballads, "real-life" memoirs, and one jerky photoplay featuring Broncho Billy Anderson and an unbilled William S. Hart, I haven't learned anything more than I knew when I read four columns in the *Fort Smith Elevator* written by a journalist named Fairclough in August 1881. His

21

account was based on interviews with Bliss and Whitelaw's acquaintances and eyewitnesses to the gang's depredations.

Lorenzo Bliss, the accidental issue some twenty years before of a business transaction between an Irish federal quartermaster sergeant named Bliss and a Mexican whore called Cincuenta Maria, or Fifty Times Mary, had fled Amarillo around age thirteen after taking off the head of one of his mother's customers with a shotgun. Like other desperadoes before and after him, he sought sanctuary in the Nations, but did not behave himself there, either. He had been arrested twice for smuggling whiskey and escaped both times, the first by setting fire to his jail cell in Cherokee and slipping out during the confusion; the second time he managed to work himself free of his manacles while riding in the back of a wagon driven and escorted by deputy United States marshals bound for the federal court in Fort Smith, Arkansas, and used them to cave in the head of a deputy. With the deputy's pistol he shot two more officers, killing one and crippling the other, and made his way to freedom aboard one of their horses.

One of the other prisoners in the back of the wagon was Charlie Whitelaw, whose history up to that point made Bliss's read like Tom Brown's. He was the son of civilized Christian Cherokees who had hacked his parents and his younger brother to death with a splitting maul when he was eighteen, then burned down their cabin on the Canadian River in an unsuccessful attempt to destroy the evidence. When a warrant was issued for his arrest he shot the constable who came to serve it, using his father's old cap-and-ball Navy .36, shot him again in the head when he was lying on the ground, and took off on the man's horse. There was another shooting incident at a Guthrie whorehouse when the constable's horse was spotted tied up in front and a pair of city patrolmen went in to investigate; Whitelaw, who was in an upstairs room spending the money he had stolen from a peach tin in his parents' cupboard, set fire to the mattress to create a diversion and went out the window, where he was seen by a third officer stationed in the alley. Slugs were exchanged, the policeman fell, and Whitelaw made his getaway on another stolen horse.

A posse was convened. They tracked him to an abandoned cabin on the Cimarron, surrounded it, and forced him to surrender. He spent a month in the city jail, where deputy United States marshals took him into custody and loaded him in chains aboard a wagon bound for Fort Smith. Lorenzo Bliss was one of the prisoners already on the wagon. When Bliss made his break, Whitelaw accompanied him. They had been together ever since.

It was a match made in hell. Neither man had a future or a conscience, and they both liked burning things. They quickly assembled a band of like-minded individuals — these were never in short supply in the Indian territory — and spent the next five years laying a path of blood and ashes north to Canada.

The military precision of their raids led to speculation that some of their people were guerrillas trained during the late Southern Rebellion, but this might have been only the wish-dream of journalists who had missed the best days of Frank and Jesse James and the Youngers. Certainly they were well led, or they would have broken apart in confusion during their encounters with the law. They had sprung traps in Colorado, Wyoming, and Montana, and suffered only one casualty, a Creek half-breed named Swingtree; a slug from a sharpshooter's Remington fired from the roof of the Miner's Bank in Butte took off his right arm and deposited him in the territorial prison at Deer Lodge for life. If Swingtree had been a member of the James gang, the columns would have been full of stories of the leaders' attempts to rescuc their loyal minion in the face of withering enemy fire, but no such blanket got stretched for Bliss and Whitelaw. They were exciting press, but they were not heroes. Their chief claim to notoriety, at a time when it seemed you couldn't throw a dead cat between St. Louis and the Barbary Coast without hitting a daylight bandit, was the targets they chose. The Jameses and Youngers only robbed banks and trains. Bliss and Whitelaw destroyed whole towns.

What's more, they enjoyed it. Thirty or forty dead was the official estimate of the human cost of their spree before the mess on the Saskatchewan, but when you figured in the amount they'd stolen, it came to less than three hundred dollars per corpse. Even the medical students in Chicago were offering better than that.

I began my preparations for Canada by arranging transportation. I enjoyed this just a little more than I did the idea of spending the winter north of Montana. Shoot me, I hate horses. I had bite scars on my backside that were older than some of the deputies I rode with and a broken leg going back to my cowpunching days that still gave me hell whenever the weather turned; and on the frontier it turned faster and more often than a jackrabbit. If my contribution could speed up the Great Northern's efforts to lay track across the territory and give me the chance to trade my saddle for a first-class Pullman ticket, I'd have been on my way to the Dakota line with a sledgehammer over my shoulder a long time ago.

Ernst Kindler ran the livery, but he only reported to work three days out of the week. He wasn't lazy. It hadn't taken him long to learn that he did his best business when one of his part-timers took his place. Ernst had been Judge Blackthorne's hangman until he laid down his ropes for his first love, which was tending livestock. But a lot of people were superstitious; those five years of service on the scaffold had put something in the old man's eyes — or taken it out, no one was sure which — that made them decide they could get along without a horse or a trap for another day or two until Lars Nördstrom or Cracker Tom Bartow reported for work. I was under no such constraint. I trusted

Kindler's knowledge of animals as I did Blackthorne's understanding of statute, and anyway there were people who said the same thing about my eyes that they did about his. Also I liked to watch him tie knots.

I found him doing just that next to the barrel stove in his reeking little office. It took him all of five minutes to enter his day's transactions in the ledger, giving him the rest of the twelve hours to pluck his prodigious eyebrows, read the Bible — he was not God-fearing, but during his tenure as executioner he had made it a point to attend every trial that might end in hanging, and claimed that nothing but Kings I and II could compare to the testimony he'd heard for sheer harrowing detail — and practice his sailors and squares. Today he was sitting stooped over in the burst horsehair swivel next to his cracked desk, putting the finishing touches on a Gordian masterpiece nearly as big as his head. It must have consumed ten feet of tarred hemp.

"You wouldn't even have to put that around his throat," I said in greeting. "Just hit him in the head with it, and his criminal days are over."

He looked up with that dead gaze under

his thatched brow and grinned. Those customers who got along all right with his
eyes tended to lose their resolve when he
smiled. It wasn't that he had bad teeth; in
fact, he took better care of them than most
men in the higher professions, which may
have been why they made you think of
bleached white bones half hidden in the
wiry tangle of his beard. The starched
white collar he insisted upon wearing even
when he cleaned out the stables contrib-
uted to the overall impression of a dressed
corpse.

"Good morning, Mr. Murdock. I
thought at first you was a half-growed bear
standing there. They only come into town
when they're starved."

I didn't resent the bear remark. I had on
a bearskin I'd taken off a big black I shot in
the Bitterroots in '77, with a badger cap
pulled down over my ears. It was the "half-
growed" I didn't care for. You can only be
told you're not as big as Jim Bridger so
many times before it starts to tell on your
good disposition. "Why do you bother to
keep in practice, if you don't intend to go
back to work for the Judge?"

He sat back, turning the great twisted
ball around and around in his hands. He
had long, elegant fingers with callus

between them; the fingers of a painter or a concert pianist. He had been an artist in his way, never having had to hang a man twice because it didn't take the first time or left one to strangle slowly. The neck had snapped each time, clean and crisp as a shot from a carbine. "You can always trust a knot if you tie it right," he said then. "Knots ain't people."

I told him I needed a horse.

"You got a horse. You owe me two weeks' board on that claybank you brought back from New Mexico."

"That's a desert horse. I need to trade it for one that's good in snow. You know you can count on me for the bill."

"No horse is good in snow. What you need is one that ain't as bad as most. I got a mustang I can let you have for the claybank and fifty bucks."

"How is it a short-legged animal like that comes so high?"

He grinned and started pulling apart the knot. "I got it and you don't."

"How much mustang is it? I need a horse with bottom."

"Oh, it's a regular mongrel. Fellow I got it from said if he had his choice he'd be buried with it, because he was never in a hole it couldn't get him out of."

"Why'd he part with it?"

"He sunk every cent he had into a shaft that turned out to be full of water. Traded me the animal for the board he owed on it and ten bucks, took himself a room at the Merchants, and blew his brains out with a Sharps pistol."

"Let's have a look."

He set the ball of rope on the desk, got up, pulled on a stiff canvas coat, and led the way to the stalls, where a barrel stove identical to the one in the office glowed fiercely with each gust of wind that knifed its way through the chinks in the siding. The horses standing between the partitions stamped and blew clouds of steam in the lingering chill, but the fumes from the fresh manure and the animal heat itself kept the temperature above freezing. We stopped before a stall containing a scrawny-looking sorrel with a squiggly blaze on its forehead that reminded me of a snake. It had a black mane and a red glint in its eye I didn't like by half.

"Fellow called him Little Red," Kindler said.

"If I called it anything I'd call it Snake. But I don't name horses and mosquitoes." I took a fistful of its mane to steady it and peeled back its upper lip. In a lightning flash the mustang broke my grip and snapped at my hand. I snatched it back in time to avoid losing a finger, but the beast took off the top of a knuckle. "Son of a bitch."

"Teeth are fine," said the old hangman.

The horse nickered and showed its gums. Its grin reminded me of Kindler's.

I dug my bandanna out of the bearskin and wrapped it around my hand. The blood soaked through the cotton immediately. "I'll give you the claybank and ten. We'll forget about what Doc Schachter's going to soak me for the lockjaw treatment."

"You won't get lockjaw. He's clean. Fifty's the price."

"I suppose it's gelded."

"I don't traffic in stallions. I like to keep the boards on my stalls."

"Twenty."

"Talk around town is you're headed north," he said. "You can't take an ordinary horse up there this time of year unless you figure to cook and eat him when he lays down on you. An animal that will fight you is an animal that will save your life."

I looked at him. He was heartier than his gaunt frame and lifeless eyes suggested. He seldom shook hands with anyone because all those years working with ropes and counterweights had made his fingers as strong as cables, and he was afraid he'd forget himself and crush bone.

"You're selling hard for the price," I said. "If you're that keen on getting rid of it, you need to budge."

He looked away. That never happened; it was always the other person who lost in a staring contest. He ran a finger down a fresh yellow post holding the stall together. It hadn't been up more than a few weeks. "Bastard knocked down a partition last month and killed my best stepper."

"Not the gray."

"It was Parson Yell's favorite. He ain't been around to rent the calash since. Thirty-five, and I'll throw in what you owe me on the claybank's board."

"Done."

He turned back toward the office. "Let's splash some whiskey on that knuckle."

At the door I looked back at the mustang. It met my gaze, tossed its black mane, and grinned its hangman's grin.

3

Sloan McInerney, have you anything you wish to say before this court passes sentence upon you?"

"Yes, Your Excellency."

" 'Your Honor' is sufficient."

"I wish to say that if I wasn't drunk I wouldn't of done it and that I have gave up the Devil Rum for good and all. It is strong drink that has brought me to this sorry pass."

"That's a fine sentiment, but if you were truly repentant, you would tell this court what you did with the money you stole from the Wells Fargo box in your charge."

"I spent it, Your Excellency. I said that at the start."

Judge Blackthorne hooked on his spectacles and thumbed through the stack of sheets on the bench before him. "At six forty-five P.M. on Thursday, November twenty-fourth, 1881, you told Marshal Pendragon that the Overland stagecoach you were driving had been waylaid by three masked men ten miles east of Helena and that you were forced at gunpoint to surrender the strongbox containing eight hundred sixty-eight dollars and thirty-three cents. At half-past three the following morning, acting upon information supplied by an unidentified party, Marshal Pendragon arrested you in a room at Chicago Joe's Dance Hall and charged you with grand theft. A search of your person and rooms failed to discover more than eleven dollars and thirteen cents in cash. Do you intend this court to believe that in less than nine hours you managed to spend the sum of eight hundred fifty-seven dollars and twenty cents on women and whiskey?"

"I bought a cigar at the Coliseum."

Blackthorne gaveled down the roar from the gallery. When the last cough had faded he folded his spectacles and rested his hands on the bench.

"Sloan McInerney, having been tried and found guilty of the crime of federal grand theft, it is the decision of this court that you will be removed from this room to the county jail, until such time as you can be transported to the territorial prison at Deer Lodge. There you will be confined and forced to work at hard labor for not less than fifteen, nor more than twenty-five years. If upon your release you take it upon yourself to recover the money you stole from wherever you have it hidden, you will be satisfied to know that you sacrificed half your life for a wage of slightly more than one dollar per week." The gavel cracked.

As the jailers were removing McInerney, I waved to catch the Judge's eye. He crooked a finger at me and withdrew to his chambers.

It was the room where he spent most of his time when he wasn't actually hearing cases, and he had furnished it with as many of the creature comforts as an honest man could on a government salary. Walnut shelves contained his extensive and well-thumbed legal library as well as a complete set of Dickens and his guiltiest pleasures, the works of Mark Twain and Bret Harte, with space for his pipes and tobacco and cigars in their sandalwood humidors. The black iron safe where he kept petty cash and the court officers' payroll supported a portable lock rack in which his cognacs and unblended whiskeys continued to age patiently between his rare indulgences. The scant wall space left by his books and the window looking out on the gallows he had decorated with a small watercolor in a large mahogany frame of a French harbor and a moth-eaten, bullet-chewed flag on a wooden stretcher to remind him of his service in the Mexican War. He read for work and recreation in a well-upholstered leather swivel behind his polished oak desk while his visitors squirmed on the straight-backed wooden chair in front.

"Fifteen to twenty-five seems stiff," I said, when he had traded his robes for his frock coat and we were seated across from each other. "You gave Jules Stoddard less than that when he stuck up the freight office for twenty-five hundred."

"Stoddard didn't work for the freight company. I haven't a drop of mercy for traitors. Are you packed for Canada?" He never spent more than thirty seconds reviewing a judgment.

"Oskar Bundt said he'd have those new grips on my Deane-Adams by tomorrow. I'll be ready to go as soon as the weather breaks."

"I hope you lose that English pistol in a drift. All the other deputies carry Colts and Remingtons and Smith and Wessons. Six-shooters. The time will come when you wish you had that extra round."

"If five won't do it I might as well haul

around a Gatling. You've just got a thistle in your boot about the English."

"Port drinkers and sodomites." He clacked his store teeth, shutting off that avenue of discussion. "Inspector Vivian replied to my wire. His office is in Moose Jaw. He's reserved a room for you at the Trappers Inn there."

"I'm sure it's full up this time of year. This is the rainy season in Paris."

"You will of course leave such observations this side of the international border. I intend to press for Bliss and Whitelaw's extradition and would rather not bog down the process in a petty cultural squabble."

"If I were you I wouldn't lose any sleep over it until your best deputy manages to capture them both alive."

"My best deputy is in Fort Benton picking up a prisoner. In any case your responsibility is to advise the North-West Mounted Police and to offer your assistance in the fugitives' apprehension. You are not to behave as a one-man committee of public vigilance."

"When did Tim Rourke become your best deputy?"

"When you stopped listening to me. Did you hear what I just said?"

"I heard. Bliss and Whitelaw's scalps

have nothing to fear from me. I didn't know any of their victims."

He leaned back in his chair, retrieved a cigar from the humidor on the bookshelf, and used the platinum clipper attached to his watch chain to nip off the end. "That's the reason I selected you for this mission," he said. "All the men I can count on to follow my instructions to the letter have some personal stake in this manhunt. If they're allowed to go on much longer, there won't be a lawman west of St. Louis who isn't related to or familiar with someone they've killed or robbed or set fire to." He lit the cigar with a long match and blew a thick plume at the ceiling. "I'd offer you a smoke, but I know you don't indulge."

"I'm saving myself for that eight-hundred-dollar brand at the Coliseum."

"McInerney." He frowned through the smoke. "I hope Rourke doesn't take long getting back when the weather breaks. I don't trust the county jail to hold a hard-time prisoner for long."

"If all you need is someone to take McInerney to Deer Lodge, I'm your man."

"You have business in Canada."

"I'm not going after Bliss and Whitelaw knowing just what's in the papers. There's a man in Deer Lodge who knows more about them than anyone."

"If you mean John Swingtree, he won't talk. He'll die in prison."

"He might talk if I promise him a commutation."

"I can't offer that even if I wanted to. Only Governor Potts can do that."

"I didn't say I'd keep the promise."

He drew on his cigar, watching me, then propped it in the brass artillery-shell base he used for an ashtray and slid a sheet of stationery bearing his letterhead from the stack on the desk. "You'll need a letter from me before they'll let you see him." He dipped his pen.

The next day I went to see Oskar Bundt. A glum pack of city employees was at work in the street, shoveling the heavy snow into piles alongside the boardwalks. The sky was iron colored but looked less oppressive than it had for a week. We were in for a thaw.

The gunsmith, Bundt, was Scandinavian, but he could seldom get anyone to believe it. He was Finnish on his mother's side, and the line went straight back to the squat, swarthy Huns who had fled north to escape Rome's retribution after the death of Attila. That was his story, anyway, and since no one else in Helena except perhaps Judge Blackthorne had read all of Gibbon, he never had to argue the point. His low forehead, sharp black eyes in sixty-year-old creases, and cruel Mongol mouth didn't invite conflict in any case. I found him behind the counter in his shop, gouging a two-foot curl off a block of walnut that was beginning to resemble a rifle stock in the vise attached to the workbench. The tidy room with its pistols and long guns displayed on the walls and kegs of powder stacked on the floor smelled of sawdust and varnish and the sharp stench of acid. NO SMOKING signs were everywhere; one spark and the entire local shooting community would have to go all the way to Butte to have its firearms repaired. Every tool in the shop was made of brass.

When he saw me, he put down the gouge, wiped his hands on his leather apron, and took my five-shot revolver from a drawer. I took it and inspected the new grips. He'd hand checked them and stained the wood so that it matched the brown steel of the frame. "It doesn't look as if anything was done to it," I said.

"That was the idea. Five dollars."

I paid him in gold as expected. If I'd

used paper, it would have cost me eight. In addition to being the most expensive gunsmith in the territory, he was the most suspicious; whether because he thought the notes might be counterfeit or the government was going to fall and make them worthless, I was never sure. He was also the best at his craft in three territories.

He watched me load the chambers from the box of cartridges I'd brought, nodding approvingly when I filled the fifth. Neither of us had ever actually known anyone who had shot himself for failing to keep one empty under the hammer.

When I looked up, the expression on his face scared the hell out of me, until I realized he was smiling. It was a good enough specimen of a smile, nothing out of the ordinary — Ernst Kindler's graveyard grin had it beat for sheer sinister quality — but I'd never seen one on that face, and it gave me a turn. If the sun had risen out of the pit behind the Highland Meat Market where they threw away the bones and gristle, the effect would have been the same.

"I have a rifle for you," he said. "A carbine."

"I've got a carbine."

"Not like this one." He went through a

door at the end of the workbench and came back carrying a lever-action carbine with a nicked stock that had been varnished and revarnished many times.

I said it looked like a Spencer repeater.

"Looks ain't is." He thumbed aside a sliding trap in the brass butt plate, exposing an opening the size of a half dollar. "That's the end of the magazine. The tube extends all the way to the receiver. Holds thirty-four rounds. You load her on Sunday and shoot all week."

I took it from him. It was as heavy as a full-size rifle. I peered at the engraving on the receiver. "Who's Evans?"

"Company in Maine."

"What's it take?"

"Forty-four centerfire. Two-twenty-grain bullet with thirty grains of powder. This is the 1877 model. They goosed up the range since they came out with it in '71." He paused. "Buffalo Bill owns one."

"That's no recommendation. Every time a company comes out with a new weapon they present one to him for the publicity. He must have more guns than Harpers Ferry." I shouldered it and drew a bead on the Winchester advertisement tacked to the back wall. "It's like hoisting a hodful of bricks."

"All those extra rounds. If they weren't there you'd be carrying them in your saddlebags. It's yours for twenty-five."

I lowered it. "Why so cheap?"

"Company went out of business last year. No replacement parts."

"If it's so good, how come nobody bought one?"

"Too heavy, I suppose. Ladies' guns are the thing now. Muff pistols and hideouts."

I swung the lever forward and back. It moved smoothly, sliding a round into the barrel with a crisp chunk. "How much to try it out?"

"Twenty-five. I don't rent weapons."

"Gold or paper?"

"Gold if you got it."

"I don't." I pulled three notes out of my poke and laid them on the counter.

He made a face at the presidents. "How much ammo can I sell you?"

"One round ought to do it." I added a penny to the stack.

4

The weather broke during the middle of January. The overcast thinned and shredded, letting the sun through, and the mercury in the thermometer on the front porch of the Nevada Dry Goods stirred itself and climbed hand over hand above freezing. There were floods and drownings — cattle and people, including both cowboys sharing a line shack on the Rocking M south of town when the Missouri jumped its banks and swept away the log structure overnight. Butchering crews hired by the ranches set to work to process as many as possible of the beef carcasses piled in the bends of rivers before they began to rot. Steaks and roasts were cheap at the Highland Meat Market and in the restaurant of the Merchants Hotel. A cured leather hide in fine condition could be bought for the price of oilcloth.

After the thaw came the rains to batter down the drifts and transform the roads and Helena's main street, already saturated by departing frost, to ropy mud. I spent this period eating cheap tenderloin, watching teams of mules and workers hauling wagons out of the soup, and waiting for the next cold snap to make the roads passable. My greatest challenge was to avoid catching the eye of Judge Blackthorne, who not counting felons hated nothing so much as the sight of a federal employee collecting taxpayers' wages with his thumbs in his belt. He was quite capable of offering my services to the county jail as a turnkey just to get me out of his sight. I didn't mind the work, but I hated the smell of such places, the stenches of disinfectant and human misery, and as I figured to get my fill of them in Deer Lodge I restricted my loafing in public to the hours when the Judge was busy in court.

After a week the mercury started back down, although the sky remained clear, and the syrup hardened into ruts and ridges that broke axles and chipped teeth. I bought a shaggy gray from Ernst Kindler for my prisoner to ride, packed my bedroll and saddle pouches with supplies and pro-visions, threw a spare saddle and roll on the gray, and slung the new Evans over one side of the snake-faced sorrel, balancing it with my Winchester on the other. On my way to the jail I stopped in to see Blackthorne in his chambers.

"Are you taking a pack animal?" Since the brutal trek that had brought him there from Washington City, he had traveled rarely, but he was always fiercely interested in the details of departure.

"Not for this leg," I said. "After I drop off McInerney, I'll reprovision in Deer Lodge and use the gray."

"You're traveling through the Rockies. Can you carry enough for two men on only two animals?"

"Prisoners are easier to manage if you keep them hungry."

"All the other deputies are right, Page. You're a mean bastard."

Since he only addressed me by my Christian name when he was feeling tender toward me or wanted something, I didn't take the comment to heart. He scribbled a note to the head turnkey to release Sloan McInerney to my custody and I went to the door. He called my name again. He had taken down his book on Montana territorial law — ridiculously thick in view of how little time had passed since the first settlers had wandered in, but then, a lot of laws had been broken — and was bent over it, following the dense columns with the butt of his cigar.

"You will want to tread lightly around those Canucks," he said. "Some of them are still fighting the Revolution."

McInerney turned out to be entertaining company. A short Irishman, with powerful forearms and black muttonchop whiskers of the type they called "buggerlugs" in the British Army, he'd been recruited under another name into the Union infantry in County Limerick, only to learn when his ship dropped anchor in New York Harbor that Lincoln was paying for volunteers. He dived overboard, swam to shore, and signed up again, using the name McInerney. His intention was to desert and open a saloon with his recruitment money, but he lost it all at cards the first night and wound up fighting in three major battles, collecting a ball in his right leg at Chancellorsville that still gave him trouble when it rained or snowed. He confided to me that he was still wanted in Virginia under his original name for an indiscretion he had committed while drunk following Lee's surrender, but he neither identified the nature of the charge nor told me the name. The incident was serious enough to drive him west, where he'd made his living as a bullwhacker, mule-skinner, and finally Overland stagecoach driver, in which capacity his weakness for Mammon had placed him at Judge Blackthorne's mercy. He told these stories on horseback and across campfires with a light in his eye and a good ear for dialect that shortened the trip through the pass into the Deer Lodge Valley. He regretted nothing, including the prospect of spending the last good part of his life behind bars. For this reason I took pains to inspect his manacles often and stretch a rope from his ankle to mine when we slept, to awaken me whenever he stirred. He was too cheerful to have ruled out escape.

He made his move three days out of Helena. We'd stopped to water the horses in a runoff stream, and he squatted in a stand of scrub cedars to move his bowels. I'd been watching his hat for a couple of minutes before I realized he wasn't wearing it any more; he'd slipped it off while I was distracted by the animals and propped it up on a branch.

I backed the horses onto the bank, hitched them to a cedar, and squeaked the Evans out of its boot. He'd left a clear trail in the snow — not because he was clumsy or stupid. I followed it for a while, letting him think he'd outsmarted me, then cut back through the trees and shot off his bootheel while he was trying to mount the snake-faced sorrel. He went down on one hip and curled himself into a ball. I went over and gave him a kick.

"You make a better impression than you thought," I said. "You didn't convince me you were empty-headed enough to make your break on foot in mountain country."

He stood up, brushed off the snow, and scowled at his ruined boot. "You're good with that trick rifle."

"I've been meaning to take a practice shot since we left town."

"You mean that's the first time you fired it?" He was staring at me with his eyebrows in his hairline. "How'd you know the sight wasn't off?"

"It is, a little. I was aiming higher." I handed him his hat.

He didn't make a second try.

Deer Lodge was a ranching town, the harness shops and feed stores built of logs on perpendicular log foundations like rafts, with a main street wide enough to turn a wagon around in and the usual assortment of loafers in pinch hats and spurs holding up the porch posts in front of the saloon. The penitentiary, altogether a more substantial construction, occupied twelve acres outside the limits. Three years and fifty thousand dollars in the making, it was built entirely of native granite up to the pitch-pine roof, with bars in the windows made of iron imported from the States, wrought and set by skilled workers brought in from as far away as California. The additional cost had restricted the facility to fourteen small cells, in which at present some twenty-four men were serving out their time stacked on top of one another like ears of corn in a rick. The stink of so much humanity encased in clammy stone reached to the office of the warden, a young Irishman named McTague, whose sober dress and dour face suggested he'd come from an entirely different part of the island from his newest prisoner, whose aborted escape attempt had done nothing to dampen his affability. As I signed off on McInerney I wondered how long all that formidable construction material would hold his unquenchable spirit.

When the captain of the guard had removed McInerney, I showed Judge Blackthorne's letter to the warden. McTague read it with a frown.

"Swingtree is a recalcitrant," he said. "Last month he bit a guard during a fight in the exercise yard. He's been in the hole four weeks."

"How is the guard?"

"The stitches come out tomorrow, but I fear he's ruined for the work. I can't let you see Swingtree until he's finished his time in the hole."

"How much time did you give him?"

"Two months."

"I can't wait that long. I'm expected in Canada."

"The regulations are clear in a case like this."

I tapped the letter on his desk. "Judge Blackthorne is a presidential appointee. He has seniority over the governor in this territory, and he certainly has authority over you."

"My instructions come from the governor. He can take it up with him." He pushed the letter toward me without expression.

After a pause I picked it up and refolded it. "I hope you're this determined when a hundred or so more convicts show up at your door from the court in Helena."

"I'm afraid I don't understand." But his eyes said he did.

"Blackthorne's an old political in-fighter. He can look at a situation from all sides and decide whether a suspended sentence or a hundred and eighty days in Deer Lodge serves the public better, or if a murderer is to hang in Helena or die of old age in the territorial prison. Which way he leans might have serious bearing on your problem with overcrowding. I understand you missed a major riot by a hair a few years ago."

A tiny vein stood out on his left temple; aside from that he might have been deliberating over whether to visit the barber today or put it off for a week. "Are you speaking for Judge Blackthorne or yourself?"

"I'm an officer of his court."

A silent moment crawled past, during which the stench from the cells entered the room like a third party. At the end of it he held out his hand. I laid the letter in it and he spread it out and scribbled beneath Blackthorne's signature: OK. T. MCTAGUE. He handed it back. "Go to the end of the hall and knock on the door. Captain Halloran will take care of the details."

"Thank you."

"I hope you're careful in your responsibilities, Deputy. It's a sad thing whenever a former law enforcement officer enters this house in chains. They are in for a bad time of it from the inmates as well as the guards."

5

Halloran, the captain of the guard, was a short, thick hunk of carved maple with his head sunk between his shoulders and the look of a prizefighter beginning to go to seed. His belly had started to loosen, cinched in with his belt, and bits of steel gray glinted where he had shaven his hair close to the temples. His faded blue eyes had all the depth of tacks holding up a wanted poster.

His lips moved behind his handlebars as he read Judge Blackthorne's letter and Warden McTague's brief addendum, then without a word he stood aside from the iron-reinforced door for me to pass through into the corridor that led to the cells. He locked it behind us with a key on a brass ring as big around as a lariat and led the way between walls of sweating granite, lit by barred windows set eight feet above the floor and fifteen feet apart. The place held the dank, earthen smell of a neglected potato bin.

At length he unlocked another iron-bound door and let me into a tiny room containing only a yellow oak table carved all over with initials and a pair of split-bottom chairs that might have come from different hemispheres for all they matched. A dim shaft of gray light fell through yet another high barred window I could have covered with my hand onto a dirt floor trod as hard as bedrock.

"I'll have your sidearm," Halloran said.

I hesitated, then unholstered the Deane-Adams and offered it to him butt first.

"Sit on this side, with your back to the door." He shook the cartridges out of the cylinder into his palm, pocketed them, and threaded the revolver's barrel under his belt. "Off to the left is best, out of the crossfire."

He went out and shut the door. A key rattled in the lock.

I was alone long enough to wonder if an old warrant that was still out on me in Dakota had found its way to the warden's office. I fell to calculating how much time had to pass before the Judge realized I hadn't made it to Canada and traced me to Deer Lodge; my head was full of arithmetic when the key rattled again and the door sighed on its hinges.

John Swingtree was smaller and more frail-looking than his reputation suggested; but then, the recent amputation of an arm might have had something to do with the latter. His head was shorn so close I could see the muscles working in his scalp, his ears stuck out. The hollows in his cheeks and the deep set of his eyes left nothing to the imagination about the configuration of his skull. The skin stretched over it was the color of terra cotta, the only visible inheritance from the Creek side of his family.

None of this meant anything in relation to what he was and what he had done and could do if given his freedom. For that I looked to the hardware that accompanied him. An iron belt encircled his waist, secured with a padlock the size of a stove lid, with a manacle attached that prevented him from bending his left elbow. The manacle on the other side was empty; the vacant sleeve of his striped tunic was folded and pinned to the shoulder. A pair of chains clipped to the belt hung to iron cuffs welded about both ankles and linked together with another length of chain that forced him to walk with a shuffle, the thick soles of his shoes rasping the floor with the chain dragging between them; the sound set my teeth on edge, like someone sliding a coffin. The arrangement put me in mind of a Bengal tiger I had seen pacing its cage in a traveling show in Denver. I'd thought at the time that I'd have been less impressed with its savagery if we'd met face to face in the woods, without all that iron standing between us. It didn't mean I wasn't grateful for the iron.

Halloran, who came in behind him, had acquired a hickory truncheon since we'd parted, two feet long, three inches thick, and polished to a steel sheen. He steered the prisoner around the table with the stick resting on Swingtree's right shoulder — it would be the most sensitive — and applied pressure as if the push were needed to seat him in the chair opposite mine. Only then did he withdraw the truncheon. He stepped out into the corridor and swung the door shut with enough force to dislodge a stream of dust from the seam where the rock wall met the pitch-pine rafters. The lock clunked. There was no sound of footsteps going away. I could feel him watching us through the square barred window in the door.

A sour smell of unwashed flesh filled the room. There were no bathtubs in the hole, just an open latrine and the sound of one's own pulse. And absolute darkness; even the weak light we were in made the man in chains blink. His coarse cotton uniform was clean, so he had probably spent the last four weeks naked as well. When they chose not to hang you, they made you be good.

"Your name is John Swingtree?" The question broke a silence as hard as the granite that surrounded us.

Another silence, just as hard, filled the break. His vocal cords were rusty.

"Not in here," he said.

A swelling around his left eye gave his face a lopsided look. Nearly a month had passed since his tussle with the guards and he still hadn't healed completely. I could only guess how many welts and bruises were concealed by the uniform.

"I'm Murdock, deputy United States marshal. I've got a badge if you care to see it."

"Why'd you lie about a thing like that?"

I searched the gaunt face for some sign of amusement. It looked like a place where smiles went to die. I asked him if he wanted to talk about Butte.

"Nice town," he said. "Up to a point."

"The point where you got shot?"

His eyes went to his empty sleeve, an involuntary movement. He snatched them back. They had begun to adjust to the light. "Them rolling-block rifles are built for buffalo. A Winchester would of did as good and I'd still have both wings."

"You were robbing the bank. I don't suppose he had time to make a better choice."

"I never robbed no place. I take care of horses. I got horse blood in my veins. My grandfather stole a thousand horses from the Comanche."

"The man with the Remington didn't know that. All he knew was someone was hollering that the bank had been robbed, and a dozen or more men were galloping away, busting caps at everyone that stood between them and the town limits. You were the one he got a bead on."

"I have a bad spirit."

As he said it, his face showed expression for the first time. He wasn't being ironic or avoiding the subject. He was addressing the issue of why that bullet had found him while all his companions had ridden free, addressing it with the resignation of a man who had been born blind or deaf or deformed. Then the expression was gone, evaporated like a drop of water in a desert.

"You and your spirit might have had a better chance if Bliss or Whitelaw or any of the others had bothered to stop and give

59

you a hand up. They left you there to die."

"Only I didn't."

"No thanks to them," I said. "Thanks to them the U.S. government is going to bury you inside these walls when your time comes. What's left of you."

He said nothing.

I joined him in that for the better part of a minute, which in those surroundings you timed with a calendar. During that time I discarded entirely the idea of offering him a break on his life sentence. He wouldn't have believed it even if it were true. He had retreated into a redoubt where hope of any kind was as destructive as bullets. That came from the part of him that was Creek. You could take everything away from an Indian, even his life, but you couldn't destroy him the way you could a white man, because when you stepped back to give him room to imagine anything less than the worst, he didn't take it. What had seemed natural when I discussed it with Judge Blackthorne in his chambers faded away in that dim cell.

"Bliss and Whitelaw are in Canada," I said. "They looted a village on the Saskatchewan and burned it to the ground. I'm on my way up there to give the Mounties a hand tracking them down. You

60

know that will happen. All we have to do is follow the trail of burned buildings and corpses. You can shorten it and get in a lick for what they did to you in Butte."

"Why should I shorten it? Every less person left breathing on the outside makes rotting in here a little easier."

I sat back and folded my arms. I knew that would irritate him. His would be going numb with the elbow locked straight. "Do you think your name ever comes up when they're talking? More than likely it doesn't. They've forgotten you. Maybe not, though. Maybe thinking about you spread out in the dust with your arm stuck on by a thread makes them laugh. Did they ever laugh about the people they killed? My bet is they did. They've killed more times in five years than the Jameses and Youngers did in fifteen — and stolen a whole lot less money. They have to be getting something out of it. What do you want to bet they serve you up with all the rest when they're stretched out around a fire up north?"

"What do you want?"

He snapped out the question at the heels of my little speech. I was surprised and a little disappointed; I'd begun to build up some respect for him, and what I'd said

61

had seemed pretty transparent even to me. But then I hadn't been left naked in a black hole for twenty-eight days with nothing but my thoughts for company.

"I've read everything the newspapers have to say about Bliss and Whitelaw," I said. "It didn't take long, and most of what I read I didn't believe. Journalists are just liars who can spell. I wouldn't go lion hunting without knowing first what they eat and where they sleep. The only one who can tell me that is another lion."

"You don't have to know how to spell to know how to lie. I could just stretch a parcel of blankets and finish out my time in the hole entertaining myself thinking about you trying to wrap yourself up in them."

"You could. You won't. You hate your old partners a deal more than you hate me."

"I only just met you," he said. "I been hating the law all my life. That's a big hate and I won't have no trouble at all fitting you in."

I unfolded my arms and rested them on the table. "Why don't you just start talking and let me worry about sorting out the lies from the gospel."

"I got to warn you, I'm pretty good."

But he wasn't listening to himself. His eyes had retreated even farther back into his skull, searching the darkness there for glittering bits of the past. "I was running with these boys from Texas, not one of them worth the sweat it took to chop 'em up for compost. Fat Tom was always blowing about how tight he was with Lorenzo Bliss back in Amarillo. Johnny Dollar bet him a double eagle Bliss didn't know him from Garfield. Well, everybody but the law knowed Bliss was catching up on his whoring in Buffalo, so we drifted down there to see him call Fat Tom a liar and maybe hook up with his outfit.

"The barkeep in this rathole where we wound up pointed out Bliss drinking under a big sombrero at the back table. Fat Tom told the rest of us to stay put at the bar till he gave Lolo the office and wobbled on over. Lolo, that's what anyone called him that called him at all, though we didn't know that then; we thought Fat Tom was just being Fat Tom. The two of 'em started talking low, and I don't know what Tom said, but knowing him I reckon he was jackass enough to say something about Bliss's mother being a whore — you know, to poke his memory about how they knowed each other — because Lolo stood up with a big old bowie in his hand and just kind of gutted Fat Tom like a catfish. I remember he give the knife a twist when he pulled it back out and Tom's heart came out with it. It didn't look near big enough for a big fat man like Tom, just a mess of red gristle no bigger than a potato. Anyway somebody started hollering for the law and we all cleared out. We all happened to head in the same direction. You could say I came to run with Bliss and Whitelaw on Fat Tom's introduction."

"I thought they'd be more particular."

"Well, they was just getting started. I reckon now they ask for letters of character."

"It doesn't sound like Bliss's temper has cooled down since Amarillo. What about Whitelaw's?"

"Oh, Charlie's the thinker. He put up with his family for eighteen years before he got around to hacking them to pieces. Fat Tom might have lived another thirty minutes if it was Charlie in that saloon."

"My guess is Whitelaw does all the gang's planning."

Swingtree nodded animatedly. He was enjoying himself now. "If it was up to Lolo, he'd gun everybody in sight, then turn out their pockets for change. But don't get to thinking that means he don't run the ball when it opens. He's got the reflexes of a diamondback. Charlie'd be dead a hundred times over if it wasn't for Bliss. He is always thinking when he ought to be doing."

"Jack Sprat."

It was an absentminded comment; I didn't expect an unlettered 'breed to pick up on the reference. But his mother must have read to him, because he bobbed his head up and down again and his eyes had come back from the shadows, nut brown and bright.

"They are hell together," he said. "They wasn't nothing till they met, just a couple of bad hats rolling along, waiting for somebody to stomp 'em flat. Split them up and that's what will happen. Only you'll get dead trying to split them up."

Captain Halloran entered. "On your feet, 'breed. One more minute's another week in the hole past your two months."

I wanted to hit him with the table, and I might have if I thought I were going to get anything out of Swingtree that was as good as I'd gotten. (I might have anyway, for no other reason than that the Hallorans of this world could only be thus improved.) But I was in a good mood, and I let him take the prisoner out the way he'd brought him in.

The mood faded when I spotted a second guard standing in the corridor. He was half Halloran's age, barely more than a boy. The smooth brown barrels of his sawed-off shotgun made him older.

"What was that story about sitting outside the crossfire?" I asked. "Either one of those barrels would kill us both."

There was no humor behind the captain's handlebars. "We don't get a lot of time to practice our marksmanship."

6

The clerk who filled my order for bacon, beans, flour, and coffee at the general mercantile, a goat-faced Scot named Kilmartin, informed me my best route to Canada from Deer Lodge lay along the Rocky Mountain Trench, a trough of lowland between the Flathead Mountains to the west and the Swan and Galton Ranges to the east. He traced the path with a thick-nailed forefinger on a map tacked to the back wall that might have been drawn up by Lewis and Clark.

"That takes me thirty miles out of my way, with the Rockies still to be crossed," I said. "What's to stop me from cutting through that creek pass up north? After that it's all tableland."

"That's Métis country. You know Métis?"

"French Indians. I had a transaction with one in Dakota a few years back. I never did work out if he was Christ or Satan."

"That sums up the breed. Talk is they're fixing to go to war with Canada again over land. When the Mounties crack down, which they're bound to do anytime, the Métis will bolt back this side of the border to regroup. I would not want to be in their path when they do."

"I heard it was the Cree making all the trouble."

"Aye, them as well. Their aim is to stop the Canadian Pacific from laying track through buffalo country. If they attack at the same time as the Métis, there won't be Mounties enough to go around. You're sure you don't want to winter in Montana?"

"I'm sure I do. But I haven't put aside enough to retire just yet. How high is the creek in that pass since the thaw?"

"I've not heard. With luck ye'll drown. Them frog Injuns like to take their time with captured lawmen."

I paid him for the provisions and the advice, loaded the gray, and struck out for the pass that led to the tableland.

It was bone cold but dry. The sky was a sheet of bright metal, with the Rockies' white-capped peaks bumped out on this side as if an angry god had kicked in the sheet with his foot on the other. I'd brought along a small pot of lampblack and smeared it beneath my eyes to cut down on the glare. Tiny icicles pricked inside my nose, but there was no wind, and the sun lay across my shoulders like a warm shawl. I rode with my bearskin unbuttoned until dark, when the chill came in with the suddenness of night in the mountains. My fingers were numb, and my hands were shaking uncontrollably when I finally got a fire going. Every time I started a long trek in the northern winter, I had to learn all over again what I'd known most of my life. *Live and learn,* my father, the trapper, used to put it. *Die dumb.*

I got up at first light with every muscle in my body screaming, fed the horses, fried bacon in the skillet I'd been carrying for ten years — stolen, along with a couple of other things, from my last ranch job in lieu of two months' pay — poured boiling coffee down my throat, and picked my way through the foothills along Salmon Trout Creek, shining like quicksilver with splinters of ice glinting in the swift current. The debris along the banks told me I'd missed a honey of a flood by a week or so, but it was still swollen. In places only a strip of level ground three feet wide separated the shoulder of a hill from the water and I got off and led the sorrel mustang and the shaggy gray to avoid a bath. I don't swim any better than the odd petrified stump. I reached the pass around noon, and by the time dusk rolled in I was in the tablelands with nothing between me and the Dominion of Canada but a hundred miles of Montana Territory.

I made good time my first day clear of the pass, but a fierce squall late the next morning forced me into the lee of an old buffalo wallow to wait it out. The flakes, flinty little barbs of ice, swarmed in the gusts — at one point I swore they were blasting from four directions at once — and swept away sky and earth in a white wipe. I hobbled the sorrel and the gray to prevent them from drifting before the wind, turned up the bearskin's collar, tugged down the badger hat, tied my bandanna around the lower half of my face, and sat hugging my knees with my back against the wallow's north slope, breathing stale air and putting the devil's face on the cue ball that had shot me to this remote pocket of the earth. I fought sleep, but I must have lost, at least for a few minutes, because I dreamed that a blizzard hit Helena so hard and stayed on for so long that Judge Blackthorne was forced to chop up his billiard table for firewood.

By then the squall had passed, leaving me tented with snow to my knees. I stood and shook it off. The brief storm had spread a white counterpane from horizon to horizon; even the firs and cedars were bent like old men beneath its weight. The horses, stupid, pathetic creatures, had managed despite their hobbles to move a hundred yards away from the shelter of the slope. The ice caused by their own spent breath had pulled their lips back from their teeth to form death's-head grins. It fell away in sections when I tapped it with the butt of the Deane-Adams. I fed them handfuls of oats to restore their body heat, stroking their necks and telling them in soothing tones that I was going to sell them for steaks to the first starving Indian I met. Only the mustang appeared to understand. Its eyes went hard as marbles and it snickered.

The rest of that day was an uphill push through drifts nearly as high as my stirrups. It was just a taste of the country I was headed for, where the snow fell twice as hard for days instead of minutes, and the wind struck with the force of God slamming shut the pearly gates.

★ ★ ★

I came across my first fence the afternoon of the next day. It was four strings of barbed wire without a gate in sight, but I was pretty sure I had drifted off the road. I turned in what seemed a likely direction, followed it for several miles, and was beginning to think I'd made the wrong choice when I spotted smoke from a chimney.

The chimney belonged to a small cabin built of pitch-pine logs with a steep shake roof stacked with snow. Behind it, three times as large, stood a barn with proper siding, altogether a more expensive construction; but then, it was built to shelter wheat, not just people. A plank sign leaned against the post to the left of the gate before the house. I had to take one foot out of its stirrup and kick loose the snow to read the hand-painted legend:

**DONALBAIN FARM
BUYERS WELCOME
TRESPASSERS SHOT
MARAUDEURS ETRE FUSILLE**

I leaned down to unlatch the gate and started through, leading the gray.

"Turn right around, ye damn toad-eating savage!"

I drew rein and slacked off on the lead. I couldn't remember when was the last time I ate a toad, but since a greeting like that is generally backed up with something more substantial than invective, ignoring it did not seem the best course.

The sun was just above the log shack and square in my eyes. I shielded them with my forearm. There was a shrunken solid something under the overhang of the porch, a little darker than the shadows, vaguely man shaped; and it was holding something at shoulder height.

"This here's a Springfield musket," said the man on the porch. "If ye don't turn around right noo, I'll put a fifty-eight-caliber ball straight through you and knock doon a barn in the next county over."

Well, you have the idea. His Scots brogue was heavy enough to sink to the bottom of a peat bog. It's as hard to spell as it is to read, so I'll lay that part to rest.

"Hold on," I called out. "I'm a federal officer."

There was a silence long enough to make the horses fiddle-foot to stay warm.

"Say something more!" demanded the man on the porch.

"To hell with this. It's too goddamn cold to sit here and make a speech." I started to back the sorrel around.

"Come on ahead," he said then. "Ye don't sound like no frog I ever heard."

Close up, he was a brown and gnarled fencepost of a man in a faded flannel shirt and heavy woolen trousers held up with suspenders. A black Quaker beard ringed his seamed face and bright, birdlike eyes glittered in the shadow of his shaggy brows. When he got a good look at me he lowered his weapon, which wasn't a Springfield at all but a Henry rifle with a brass receiver.

"Whoever sold you that firearm was pulling your leg," I said.

"I traded the musket for the Henry and a case of ammunition in '78. I made worse mistakes but not lately. If ye wasn't what you said ye was and ye'd known the ball wouldn't reach the damn gate, I'd be deader'n Duncan." He screwed up his face, bunching it like a fist. "Ye got papers?"

"No papers." I had the badge ready. I tossed it to him. He caught it one-handed — a surprise, for I had him pegged at past fifty — looked at the engraving, and tossed it back. "It don't mean much, but I'm satisfied you ain't one of them damn blood-sucking Métis."

I didn't pursue that. "I'm bound for Canada. If you let me camp on your property tonight and cut through in the morning I'll thank you."

He scratched his chin through his whiskers. "Feed you supper for a dollar."

"I'll make my own."

"No sense us both eating alone," he said after a moment. "You can bed down your animals in the barn. Spread your blanket there. I'll fill the basin out back of the house. I got a pot of venison stew on the stove. That's my dollar's worth of good works for law and order." He uncocked the Henry.

"The sign means what it says. Buyers are welcome; the wheat or the farm, it don't matter which. I lost my taste for the life when my Marta died."

The orange glow from the coal-oil lamp on the table filled the lines in Donalbain's features, increasing his resemblance to the young man in the sepia-tinted wedding photograph that hung on the wall behind him in an oval frame. We were drinking sherry from an old green bottle, using barrel glasses with bottoms as thick as sadirons. The venison stew sat pleasantly in my stomach.

"Is that when you took up French?" I asked.

"I got it out of one of Marta's books. She was a teacher in Boston when I met her."

All of the cabin's decorations, including the rag rug and linen shelf linings, obviously predated his wife's death. The air was a stale mulch of woodsmoke, tobacco, coffee beans, damp wool, kerosene, and rank male. Sooty cobwebs hammocked the rafters. Loneliness hung as heavily as the carcass of an old bull buffalo.

"You translated 'trespassers shot.' Why not 'buyers welcome'?"

"There ain't a Métis alive who's begged or stole enough to meet my price. And they're the only ones around who read French. I translated the one I needed."

"They told me in Deer Lodge the Métis are getting ready to declare war on Canada."

"They'll just lose their shirts like they did the last time. Then they'll come back down here begging and stealing and making life hell all over again for the honest. I've found it's easier to blow them out of their moccasins than talk to them at all." He refilled our glasses from the bottle.

He'd emptied his three times since we'd started drinking, and his speech and his hand were as steady as when he'd had me under the gun. "Don't tell me the government's taking an interest in them after all this time."

"No, I'm chasing a couple of fugitives. You might have read about them: Lorenzo Bliss and Charlie Whitelaw."

"I don't take the papers. They're full of lies. Murderers, are they?"

I nodded. "They've run out of laws to break in the United States. The prevailing thought seems to be the Mounties need my help stopping them before they start on the North Pole."

"Know them well, do ye?"

"I haven't had the pleasure."

He drank, tipping the glass at a careful angle to prevent sediment from stirring from the bottom. His eyes never left me. "Ye'll not take offense when I say ye don't look like that such of a much."

"There's more to me than meets the eye. Except when it comes to billiards."

"Billiards?"

"It's a story I don't feel like telling."

"Golf's my game, or was before I left Benmore at the request of the queen's soldiers." He reached for the bottle, shook it, and thumped it back down with a scowl. "I'd not insert myself betwixt the Cree and the damned Métis and the railroad for all the wheat in Montana. They won't welcome ye, and neither will the North-West Mounted. Those redcoats have had the run of that country going on ten years. They don't answer to Ottawa nor the Colonial Office in London, though they'll no admit it. They'll take tea with ye Monday, push ye off a mountain Wednesday, and write a letter to Chester Arthur Friday with their regrets. But ye'll no have to concern yourself with any of that, because long before ye get on the hair side of them the winter up there will kill ye like spring grass."

7

I crossed into Canada a week out of Deer Lodge. Or so I thought.

There were no signs or checkposts, and the climate and scenery didn't change. But something happens to my body whenever I enter foreign country — a lifting of the hairs and a heightened sensitivity in the skin, that I learned long ago not to ignore. I had no official papers apart from Judge Blackthorne's letter introducing me to Inspector Vivian of the North-West Mounted, and I almost never wore the badge, but I'd been in possession of it for so long I felt the exact moment when I stopped being a lawman and reverted to private citizen. I had a sudden, giddy urge to keep on riding, all the way to the uncharted territories, where I could build a cabin on some river loaded with trout and beaver and never have to worry about serving another warrant. Then I remembered I'd left the wilderness to get away from trout and beaver in the first place, and stopped to ask a gang of loggers clearing timber for the Canadian Pacific for directions to Moose Jaw.

The foreman, short and thick in a woolen shirt and trousers, lace-up boots, and a red stocking cap, leaned on his ax and built a cigarette. "Shortest way is through that gap in the pines," he said. "You will want to go the long way, north to the river and follow it east."

He had a husky French accent, but there was no Indian in his puffy, black-bearded face. He wasn't Métis.

"Why would I want to do that?" I asked.

"The short way takes you through Cree country."

"Are they fighting?"

"Not yet. But I would not wish the honor of being the first white man to die."

"I'm surprised you're not posting guards."

"There is a rifle trained on you from up in that lodgepole on the ridge."

A sparse stand of tall pine topped a rise to the west, one of them taller than the others. After a moment I made out a dark bulk high in the branches. "He must be part tree frog," I said.

"He is American, like you. He was, how you say, a sniper in your Civil War for two years." He put a match to his cigarette and cocked his head to keep the smoke out of his eyes, watching me.

"Which side?"

"I have forgotten. They are all the same."

There was a time when I would have given him an argument. But it had been seventeen years. Stone's River seemed like something that had happened to someone else.

"What makes you think I'm American?" I asked.

"Because you are going the short way."

I looked him in the eye, and he saw in mine that he was right. I thanked him for the information and started for the open space in the line of trees to the east.

Saskatchewan, which was where I judged myself roughly to be, had either enjoyed a mild winter so far or had experienced a thaw about the same time as Montana, or the snow would have been deeper; that north country tending as it did to pile snowfall upon snowfall until settlers had to dig tunnels between their houses and outbuildings. Whenever the freeze had come, it had been in effect long enough to freeze the ground as hard as iron. Wherever the wind had scraped out a bare spot, the horses' shoes rang like a blacksmith's shop during the busy season. The flakes that were falling about me were large and cottony and made no sound when they landed. I rode through ten miles of forest hearing nothing but the creak of my saddle and the horses blowing steam.

I saw no Indians the first day. That meant nothing, not that they had any reason to hide in their own country, and from a lone rider; they were so much a part of the landscape that I would have had to concentrate hard to see them, just as it would have taken me a minute to spot a thirty-year bookkeeper in a room full of ledgers. But I had grown up in Blackfoot territory, had a pretty good eye, and was convinced that if there were any Cree close by, they weren't interested enough in one man on horseback leading a pack animal to brace him, kill him, or show themselves. When I reached a cut of swift black water I guessed was the Moose Jaw River, near dusk, I made a bit of noise breaking up pine boughs for firewood and built a nice big fire with plenty of smoke. In bear country, you make it a point not to startle the big brutes by sneaking up on them, and it's not all that different with Indians. They might make fun of you for your clumsiness and for burning too much fuel for one man, but at least they didn't consider you a threat. It was a theory, and if it explained why so many fools and tenderheels passed unscathed through ground that had claimed men wiser and more seasoned, it was worth a try.

My chance to test it came earlier than I'd hoped.

I'd broken camp shortly after first light and had secured everything aboard the gray except the skillet, which I'd left in the snow to cool, when I heard the measured creak of stealthy hooves setting themselves down in the fresh fall. I didn't think it was the loggers. They had no reason to come this way unless they were clearing timber, and I'd ridden beyond earshot of their saws and axes half an hour after I talked to the foreman. There were few ranches in that wooded country, so it wasn't line riders. Wolfers possibly, hunting pelts for bounty.

I clung to that last thought, because it gave me the sand to turn my back on the sound as if I hadn't heard it. I strode over to the skillet, scooped it up by its handle, and started back toward the horses as if I were going to slip it into a pack. When I had the animals between me and my visitors, I let go of the skillet and veered toward the snake-faced sorrel. Fortunately the Winchester was hanging on my side; it had a true sight, unlike the Evans, and I knew what to expect of it in the heat of a fight. I slid it out of its scabbard, levered a round into the chamber, and laid the barrel across the throat of my saddle, all in one movement.

The riders kept on coming at the same pace, just as if I were still holding the skillet instead of a carbine. At a distance of a hundred yards they didn't look much like Indians. The one nearest me had on a mackinaw and his five companions wore bearskin and buffalo coats and one canvas jacket trimmed with fleece, the kind of variety commonly found among parties of white men out hunting or searching for stray cattle. Two of them were wearing hats. There wasn't anything about them to suggest Indian from where I stood, except their formation.

White men could live outdoors for years and never manage the shapeless, scattered quality of a group of nomadic tribesmen traveling together on horseback. The party looked as if it might break up at any time, one or two or all of the riders deciding to abandon the others on some whim and strike out on their own. That was the point. One sign of trouble and they vanished in several directions, like smoke in the wind. Fire into a tight pack and you were bound to hit something, but if your first bullet didn't find a target in this bunch you might as well shoot at fog. I fixed my sights on the one in the mackinaw and waited while the band approached at a casual pace, trickling between and around the trees like rivulets of water.

Mackinaw seemed to know the precise moment when he drew within effective range, because he raised his right hand and held it palm forward to show there was no weapon in it. The others did the same. I raised my cheek from the stock but kept the Winchester where it was, Indians being nearly as sneaky as white men and just as good about keeping their word.

They leaned back on their hackamores forty feet short of where I was standing, just as I was thinking of chugging a round into the earth at their feet to warn them against coming too close.

There followed a silence that was supposed to frighten the hell out of me. Nobody likes to talk more than an Indian, and nobody knows better the power of a pause. High up in the straight pines where the boughs grew, a small bird fluttered between branches, loud as a steam engine starting up. Even the sorrel snorted and rippled its skin. I grew roots and waited it out.

The one in the mackinaw had some years on him. Bars of silver glinted at his temples, and thinner strands wound through the braids framing his face, which was burnt umber and canted back from an impressive nose, like the corner of a building in a lithograph on a bank calendar. A beaded ornament on a leather necklace cinched in the loose skin of his neck. From there up he was all native. The rest of him would have been at home in Denver, from his trousers of tightly woven wool to his stovepipe boots smeared with grease to make them waterproof to the platinum watch chain that described a fashionable J from the right slash pocket of his mackinaw to the placket where it buttoned at his throat. I wondered if there was a watch at the end of it, and if he ever took it out and popped open the face to check the time, like a senator with a train to catch.

He carried no weapons that I could see, but he didn't have to. I counted three Springfield carbines and two Spencers among the others, tarted up with brass tacks the way they liked them, and just for old times' sake a longbow and a quiverful of arrows. None of them was trained on me. Small comfort; what the tribes back home lacked in accuracy they made up for in speed, and I had no reason to believe a line drawn on a map had any effect on that.

A minute had crawled past, and I was getting cold standing there without moving. I gave in then. Indians liked to win, and they hadn't been doing much of that since the Little Big Horn. I raised my right hand and made the Cheyenne sign that said I wasn't looking for a fight. I hoped I got it right. It had been years since I had had anything to do with Indians other than run away from them.

There was a general letup in pressure then. One of the two men in hats chuckled and said something to the other one, who nodded. A look from the one in the mackinaw and they both settled down.

Mackinaw spoke. "You are with the railway?"

It was only five words, but he rolled his *r*'s with the theatrical assurance of Donalbain the Montana farmer. He had learned his English from the Scots immigrants who had settled the area.

"No," I said. "I'm on my way to Moose Jaw on private business." I'd decided against identifying myself as a U.S. federal officer. I didn't know how much contact he might have had with the Sioux and Cheyenne who had migrated north after the Custer battle, carrying their tales of injustice at the hands of the authorities in America.

"You are American."

I was beginning to wonder if it was tattooed on my forehead. "I am."

"Why do you travel alone?"

"I'm not alone."

"It is a lie." There was no emotion in the statement. "This is the land of the Cree. You ride across it as if you own it. You lay the forest naked, tear the earth, and lay steel across it. The buffalo will not cross the steel and so the great herd is sliced in two, the easier to rub it out. Why do you do these things?"

"I'm not with the railroad," I said. "I'm on my way to Moose Jaw on private business, and this way was pointed out to me as the shortest."

"What is your business?"

I shook my head. "It's private."

He thought this over, or maybe not. Indians' faces as a rule might have been made of glass, exposing the workings of their brains, but this one was painted out.

The dark eyes traveled over my outfit.

"You must pay to cross the land of the Cree," he said then. "You have two rifles. You will give us one."

I thought that over, not knowing if he could see what I was thinking. It was standard practice to trade something for the privilege of passage through Indian territory; I had done it on more than one occasion and never missed the item, which had bought back my life. I had no special attachment to the Evans, despite the awesome capacity of its magazine. I thought about all this, and I knew as surely as I could no longer feel my feet in the cold that if I gave up so much as a spoon from my kit I wouldn't live to see noon. It was in the air, if not in the aging brave's face.

"No."

The five others exchanged glances. Even their horses — gaunt, grass-fed paints with shaggy winter coats — shifted their weight restlessly from hoof to hoof and shook their manes, blowing up clouds of steam. Only the Cree in the mackinaw remained motionless, his gaze locked with mine. I did something very difficult then. I lowered my cheek to the Winchester's stock and closed one eye, drawing a bead square in the middle of Mackinaw's chest. Dying was a little less frightening when you took along a companion.

Forepieces rattled as the Spencers and Springfields lifted into firing position. It occurred to me then I had a better chance if I shifted my sights to one of the armed warriors. I didn't. I played out the hand I'd dealt myself. The platinum watch chain made a bright target.

I was so tense I almost squeezed the trigger when Mackinaw gathered his reins.

"Do not stop again in the land of the Cree," he said.

He turned his horse then. After a moment the others followed suit, in a ragged order that would have made an Irish drill sergeant hurl his hat to the ground in frustration. Sloppy or not, in a moment the band was gone, as completely and silently as breath on glass.

I blinked. After a while I took the Winchester off cock and finished breaking camp. When I pulled out I swung the mustang past the hoofprints in the snow where the Indians had stopped, just to make sure I hadn't dreamt the whole thing.

8

You're certain it was a watch chain? Not an ornament of native manufacture that looked similar? They're devilishly clever at imitation."

The man seated behind the desk might have been in his middle thirties or his late fifties. His hair was absolutely without color, chopped close at the temples and full on top and brushed back. His square face was deeply sunburned, nearly as red as his tunic, bringing into prominence his sandy, military-cut moustache and pale eyes in which the pupils were like black specks on blue china. URBAN VIVIAN was engraved on the heavy brass nameplate on the desk, no rank or title provided.

"It was a watch chain," I said. "German, I think. At forty feet I couldn't be sure."

"It could have been any Indian bugger in a mackinaw. They've been trading with explorers and settlers since before the Revolution; I wouldn't be surprised to find an icebox in one of their tipis, with kippers

91

inside and a bottle of tawny port on top. But there's only one Cree who sports a platinum watch chain in the proper gentleman's manner. It had to have been Piapot himself."

His English accent was as brittle as his appearance. The war in the South had burned away most of my patriotic pride, but hearing him talk made me want to whistle "Yankee Doodle" just to see what he'd do. Instead I asked him who Piapot might be.

His flush deepened. "You Yanks really don't pay heed to anything that don't threaten your precious Union. Piapot's the chief of the entire Cree Nation, that's all. His warriors have been busy as teamsters pulling up survey stakes along the Canadian Pacific right-of-way for a month. Up till now we hoped it was just some disgruntled renegades, but if Piapot's in the area it means it's got his seal. Indians go their own way as a rule, and hang the chief if his interests ain't theirs. It's different with him. There are seasoned braves who have never known another leader. He might as well be jerking up the stakes with his own two hands."

I'd been with Vivian ten minutes, long enough for him to read Blackthorne's letter and hear my account of the palaver in the woods. His office was a one-story walk-up by way of an outside staircase next to a feed store. The room took up the building's entire second story, with only his desk and a work table and a row of upright wooden chairs to occupy it. A skin that must at one time have belonged to a fifteen-hundred-pound grizzly managed to look small in the middle of the plank floor. Apart from that the place resembled any city lawman's office in the American territories, complete with a row of rifles and shotguns glistening in a locked rack, a corkboard stacked with wanted readers three deep, and the obligatory blue-enamel pot boiling away on a potbelly stove that might have come from the estate of Ben Franklin. (It was a *tea*pot; but then Canada was mostly settled by people who would never forgive Boston its party.) The maple-leaf flag hanging from a standard in one corner provided a colorful change of pace, along with a gold-fringed blue banner tacked to the wall behind the desk, featuring a buffalo head beneath a coronet encircled by the legend NORTH-WEST MOUNTED POLICE. At the bottom appeared the motto MAINTIEN LE DROIT, which Judge Blackthorne had translated for me: Maintain the Right.

A pair of tall, narrow windows looked out on Moose Jaw: all two blocks of it, log and clapboard buildings with signs in English and French advertising stores (shops, they called them there), drinking establishments, and one hotel, the Trappers Inn. The street separating them was a hundred feet wide, scored and rutted and frozen as hard as granite. It had all the appearance of a town founded by trappers and Indian traders struggling to stay alive between the crash of the fur market and the coming of the railroad (railway, they called it there). The very fact that the North-West Mounted had decided to open an office there must have given the locals hope to go on.

"Why don't you bring in the British Army to deal with Piapot?" I asked.

"We don't handle things that way. Unlike your American cavalry, we've managed to learn from our mistakes."

"You wouldn't know that from your record in India and Africa."

He had a silver snuffbox on his desk. He used it, sneezing into a handkerchief he drew from his left sleeve. All he had to do now to make me like him less was hop on a pony and whack a wooden ball with a mallet.

"I was a regular army officer for twelve years," he said, tucking the handkerchief back into his cuff. "Worked my way up through the ranks. Fought in Abyssinia and at Roarke's Drift. Bloody buggers, both campaigns, and all we managed to win was the contempt of half the world's native peoples."

"And most of the African continent. Don't forget that."

He pointed a finger at me. There was an impressive callus on the end of it, but he might have gotten that from a pen. "Yes, and in the end you Yanks will have a continent as well, and spend the rest of the century fighting to hold on to it. Blood for dirt ain't a fair trade."

I had nothing to throw at that, so I withdrew from the field. "I can't feature Piapot letting me live. I had a bead on him, but I never knew an Indian to be afraid to die. The others would have chopped me to pieces before I got in a second round."

"Crees are hard to predict or explain. They respect a show of sand. Or he might have thought you were daft, which is bad medicine. You're a lucky bloke either way. You should have given up the rifle."

"If what you say is true, that might have gotten me killed."

"Perhaps. Your government doesn't have the corner on treachery."

Now we were moving in circles. "What news of Bliss and Whitelaw?"

"Nothing since that bad business on the Saskatchewan at Christmas." He relaxed a little; his shoulder blades actually touched the back of his chair. "It wasn't enough for them to steal every dollar and gold filling in the settlement. They had to take target practice on the locals as well, and put a tourch to everything that wouldn't bleed. I helped bury the bodies. Some of them were burned all in a heap, their flesh melted in one lump; rather than try to separate them we dug a big hole and pushed them in like rubble. They smelled like burnt pork. I sent to Regina for troops and we tracked the buggers as far north as Saskatoon when a blizzard wiped out the trail. They didn't pass through town. I wired the constable in Prince Albert to keep an eye out. I'm still waiting for an answer. That far up the lines are down as often as not."

"What's past Prince Albert?"

"Eight hundred miles of wilderness, clear up to Victoria Island. Beyond that's the Arctic Ocean. Oh, there's a river settlement two hundred miles north of Albert, founded by former American slaves, and a stronghold up on Cree Lake full of Sioux Indians who chose not to surrender with Sitting Bull last summer, but even Bliss and Whitelaw aren't barmy enough to take on either one. They're armed camps."

"The slaves are armed?"

"*Former* slaves — and free up here since long before Lincoln. They'll shoot a white American as soon as look at him. There's not a one of them as didn't have a wife or mother or some other close kin sold down the river at one time or another. Americans have been known to disappear in that vicinity, and there's not a Mountie in the country could track them to where they're burned or buried. The locals are always polite to redcoats, invite us in for dinner and a jug, but when we ask them what became of so-and-so, they roll their eyes and shake their heads, laughing at us the whole time behind that plantation-nigger show. I hope to blazes Bliss and Whitelaw tried them on; it would save Her Majesty the cost of a trial and Washington the price of extradition. But I don't count on it."

"What's the name of the settlement?"

"Shulamite. Not that you'll need to know it, except as the name of the place you want to ride wide around. The settlers put their trust in a hag of an African shaman, and I don't set any store by such claptrap, but she'll see straight through you if you try to brass it out and claim you're anything but a wicked slave-taking white American. I suspect her hideous old face is the last thing those men who vanished ever saw."

"How many men are riding with Bliss and Whitelaw?"

He took another pinch but didn't sneeze this time. He seemed relieved not to be still discussing Shulamite and its witch queen. "The survivors of the massacre couldn't agree on a number. As few as eight, as many as fifteen. The witnesses were in shock, and it's usual in those circumstances to count high. Enough, anyway, to call for a company of Mounties when we find out where they're hiding." He glanced down at Blackthorne's letter. "You know, I sent wires to the capitals of all the American territories where these animals committed atrocities, but Helena was the only one that offered to send help. I suppose the others think Bliss and Whitelaw are our problem now. But this letter don't say anything about how many men are coming behind you. I frankly don't care for the prospect of a gang of heavily armed strangers loitering about town, and neither will Superintendent Walsh. Such men become bored easily."

"Tell Superintendent Walsh not to worry. I'm the entire expedition."

"I'd feared that. Your Judge Blackthorne is disingenuous. He has no interest in assisting us, merely in protecting the United States' claim on Bliss and Whitelaw and their accomplices when they are apprehended. You're here in the role of a spy to see that Canada doesn't hang them first."

"Blackthorne's a low fighter," I said. "He's vain, too, and he cheats at billiards. But it won't do to run down the authorities in the other territories because they'd just as soon you dealt with the situation and then run down the Judge for saying it's his responsibility too. Bad form, I think you Brits call it."

"Only in cheap novels written by Americans." He refolded the letter, smoothing the seams with his horned fingers as if they needed it after riding folded in a saddle pouch for three hundred miles. He would do everything twice, minimum; I was betting that under his tunic he wore galluses and a belt. He said, "I can't offer you a thing beyond the quarters I arranged for you and the opportunity to submit a request for extradition once the fugitives are in custody. I shan't stop you if you volunteer to accompany any party I assemble when we receive news of their whereabouts, but I remind you that you have no official status in Queen's country. You will obey my orders. And before you leave this office you will surrender to me any firearms you have on your person. They aren't permitted in town."

I shifted my weight in the hard chair, unholstered the five shot from under my bearskin, and passed it across the desk buttfirst. "What about my rifles?"

"You can leave them with Jules Obregon at the livery when you board your horses. He'll see they're delivered here." He frowned approvingly at the revolver. "English weapon. Do you not subscribe to the popular Yankee conceit that only Sam Colt made men equal?"

"I won my first Deane-Adams off a stock detective in Kansas in '76 on a jack-high straight. He bought it back from me and then used it to try to hold me up for the rest of the pot. I shot him with the Army Colt I was carrying at the time and took the English gun for my trouble. He didn't see me palm the cartridges when I sold it to him."

"You killed him?"

"Not right away, but it's difficult to shoot someone at that range without blowing out too much to put back in."

He smoothed his moustache with a knuckle, evaluating me with those pale eyes. "I should think the incident was a better argument in favor of the Colt."

"Not really. A pistol without cartridges hasn't had a fair comparison. I liked the feel of the Deane-Adams. It took me six months to find a replacement after I lost it somewhere between Bismarck and Fargo in '78."

"Another shooting incident, no doubt."

"It's a frontier, Inspector. That's not a police whistle hanging from that peg."

He didn't bother to turn his head to look at the cartridge belt and what looked like the handle of a Russian .44 sticking out of the flap holster on the wall where he hung his white cork helmet. "I've drawn that weapon once in the line of duty since I was assigned here four years ago, to disarm a drunk. Moose Jaw isn't Tombstone. It's a wild land, but most British subjects respect the law even when they can't see it. If it weren't for your Indian wars and your expatriate desperadoes, I should be sitting in a comfortable office in Ottawa, sipping whiskey

101

and soda and discussing the fights."

"Well, I'll try and take Bliss and Whitelaw off your hands at least."

"Right." He placed the revolver and the Judge's letter in the top drawer of the desk and banged it shut. "The linen in the Trappers Inn is above reproach, but if you heed my advice, you'll sleep there only and take your meals at the Prince of Wales. I recommend the fried chicken, and I'm told the cook poaches an excellent trout. As I'm one Londoner who can't abide fish, I'm unable to offer an opinion based on experience. Is there anything else I can do to make your stay more pleasant?" He wasn't gentleman enough to bother to make the invitation sound sincere, but then he'd come up through the ranks. It cost him plenty to avoid dropping his *h*'s.

"Just one thing."

I surprised him, not for the first time, nor yet again for the last during that brief meeting. He had a leather portfolio of papers on his desk and had already begun to absorb himself in them. He looked up, brows lifted. That's when I surprised him again.

I said, "Tell me where I can find the survivors of the massacre on the Saskatchewan."

9

The lobby of the Trappers Inn was less than half the size of Inspector Vivian's office and contained twice as many fixtures and furniture. A great shaggy moose head with a six-foot antler spread seemed to breathe down my neck while I registered for the clerk, three hundred pounds of solid fat with long gray hair and no discernible gender. A pair of crossed snowshoes hung on the wall next to the stairs and a smooth-bore musket of Revolutionary War vintage decorated a ceiling beam, looking not so much like ornaments as things that were taken down frequently and used. So far everything I had seen about Canada made me feel that the entire country had been pressed between the pages of a novel by James Fenimore Cooper.

The room I got smelled suffocatingly of cedar and soiled wool with a single discolored window, a smoky fireplace, a chipped-enamel washstand, and a cornshuck mattress on a narrow iron bedstead. The sheets and pillowcases were white and freshly pressed, as Vivian had promised. After so many nights sleeping on the frozen ground, I thought it was the presidential suite at the Palmer House in Chicago. I built a fire from a box full of seasoned pine and cedar, pried the window up an inch to let the smoke out, helped myself to a swig from a bottle I'd bought in Deer Lodge, and slept for two hours without even trying.

I awoke at dusk, sore all over and hungry enough to order the moose head for dinner. Stripped to the waist, I washed with cold water and scraped off the top layer of stubble, then put on a clean shirt and went downstairs to ask for directions to the Prince of Wales. The clerk, who I guessed was some mix of French and Indian, but whose sex I still could not decide upon, looked at me with small black eyes like a mole's.

"Dining room's through that door. Tonight's pot roast of beef."

"Thanks. I asked about the Prince of Wales."

"You must be rich as Gladstone." But the clerk told me the way.

His Royal Highness might have stuck his nose up at it, but the restaurant was as civilized as anything I'd seen in months. The floor was sanded and scrubbed white, the walls were plastered and papered and hung with portraits of H.R.H. and his mother the Widow of Whitehall, and the tables were covered in white linen. The room was half full at that hour, the locals in mackinaws and woolen shirts and heavy knitted pullovers, some in stocking caps and brimmed hats with stains on the crowns where they gripped them between greasy thumbs and forefingers. Some of the diners were women, dressed like men for the most part, skirts of durable material and no particular color hanging to their boottops so that they looked like male-female combinations in a medicine show, divided halfway down. They would save their femininity for the short warm season.

I hung up my bearskin on a peg already layered with coats and scarves and found a corner table. A waiter with a shorn head and handlebars appeared while I was reading the menu. I asked for fried chicken and a bowl of mushroom soup.

"Anything to wash that down? We got red and white."

"Just water."

He went away with a shrug, a large man in a clean apron who walked on the balls of his feet like a prizefighter. He didn't take the menu. I pretended to interest myself in the breakfast bill of fare while my fellow diners stole glances at me. They would know who I was by now, small towns being the same on both sides of the border, and they would want to know if the American lawman was as tall as Pat Garrett or as curly-headed as James Butler Hickok. I wasn't either one; little by little their attention strayed back to their meals and stayed there.

The soup was good if slightly musty, made from mushrooms dried during autumn for keeping and soaked in water when they were prepared. I'd had better fried chicken in Virginia, but I could see how it would impress an Englishman like Vivian. At that moment the man himself entered, shook the snow off his flat-brimmed campaign hat and sheepskin coat with the fleece turned inside before hanging them up, and came straight my way without appearing to have looked around. Probably he had spotted me through the window. He would be the kind of man who never wanted to look as if he didn't know where he was headed, a man accustomed to being watched and who behaved accordingly. I hoped he wasn't going to get me killed.

"I see you took my advice," he said by way of greeting. "How do you like the chicken?"

"It's all right. At this point anything that doesn't taste like bacon suits me down to the ground."

His attempt at a smile soured. I'd intended to compliment him, but even when I try to say something polite to someone I don't like it comes out wrong. "May I sit down, or are you one of those blokes who prefers to dine alone, like a Neanderthal?"

"It's a free country," I said. "Whoops, no, it's not. But suit yourself."

He sat with his hands on his thighs and watched me finish off a leg. "We've started off poorly, I'm afraid," he said. "My grandfather was killed at New Orleans. What I've seen of most Americans who come up here hasn't done a great deal to eradicate the family antipathy."

"I'm surprised you came here."

"I haven't eaten since breakfast. Oh, you mean *Canada*." He bared his teeth. "Rank can be purchased in the British military, if you have the wherewithal. I bought mine with blood and sweat. The wealthy class is not overrun with idiots, but they have their share, and most of them seem to think they'd look good in brass buttons. One morning a colonel whose father was serving in the House of Lords asked me if I didn't agree that the Sikhs and Muslims ought to be able to sit down and work out their differences in the spirit of Christian good fellowship. I resigned my commission that afternoon. I was among the first three hundred Mounties dispatched to Fort Garry in '73."

He paused, then recited, in a clear, pleasant tenor that turned heads at the nearby tables: " 'Sharp be the blade and sure the blow and short the pang to undergo.' That's what the *Toronto Mail* predicted when we rode west. Nobody gave us a Chinaman's chance against the northern tribes after the massacre in Cypress Hills. And yet here we are. That wouldn't be the case if the idiots had come out with us."

"Maybe. The Army of the Potomac had more idiots than Robert E. Lee had gray hairs, but we managed to beat him anyway."

"Fought the good fight against slavery, did you?"

"I never saw a slave in my life, and neither did a good many of the men I helped kill in that war. It wasn't about slavery. I can't tell you just what it was about now, though I was pretty sure then."

"We all were," he said; and for a moment there we were thinking about the same thing, if not the same war. Then the waiter came and he ordered the chicken and a bottle of white concord. "That is if you'll join me, Deputy."

"Thanks. Wine sours my stomach."

"A glass, then." When the waiter left, Vivian drew an envelope from inside his tunic and placed it beside my plate.

I mopped the grease off my hands with my napkin but didn't pick up the envelope. "I haven't been in town long enough to acquire an admirer, and you're no messenger."

"Directions. You'll find the place inaccessible without them. I can't guarantee she'll talk to you even when you find her. But it's all I can do."

"She?"

"You said you wanted to interview survivors of the massacre. Most of them have been moved four hundred miles east to Fort Garry, to await relocation next spring to the homes they left behind, some of them in England and France. Only one elected to remain in the area. She's living in a tent on the site of the cabin she shared with her husband and two children. She won't leave their graves."

"Is she too heavy to scoop up and carry?"

"She has a shotgun and a great blunderbuss of a pistol that belonged to her husband, neither of which she is ever without. I cannot say whether she intends to use them on herself or whoever draws near enough to seize her. I'm reluctant to find out. I make it a point to ride out there every ten days or so and deliver provisions. She is always sitting Indian fashion outside the tent, with the shotgun across her lap and that big revolver strapped about her waist. I don't know if she ever goes inside. The only evidence that she moves at all is the provisions I left last time are always gone when I bring replacements. I leave them on a flat rock, outside shotgun range."

"How long's it been since the last time?"

"I was planning to make another delivery tomorrow. I cannot predict how she'll react if two men ride out there at the same time," he added.

I picked up the envelope then and took out the directions. He had a neat round hand, symmetrical if not elegant. His wrist would never touch the desk while he was writing. "What is it, about a day's ride?"

"Count on being gone two nights. It gets dark early in that thick forest."

"Mining settlement, wasn't it? Did they see much in the way of color?"

"Just enough to trade for supplies once or twice a month here in town. It's a hard life. Some trapper who hasn't got the word there's no more market for beaver pelts in London finds a nugget and they come pouring out here planning to get rich in a fortnight. If they have any luck at all they make wages. Have you ever met an old prospector?"

"Only in dime novels."

"Forty's the expected span. They die of pneumonia or starvation or fall off mountains or follow color too deep into Indian country, and no one knows what happened to them until some other twit stumbles over their bones. Partners kill each other over a handful of dust or just because they tire of staring at the same face all the time, or they kill themselves because it's easier than going home failures. Or they manage to survive all that, and a pack of animals on the run from America slaughters them for two or three hundred in raw ore. All to make an attractive setting for the diamond on Jim Brady's pinky finger."

"That's not why," I said, "and you've

been out here long enough to know that."

"Oh, I know bloody well the importance you Yanks put on your precious liberty. You'll sacrifice everyone else's to maintain the illusion."

"You English always make good points. I'll take it up with my Irish and Scot friends and get back to you."

The waiter brought his fried chicken. When we were alone, Vivian spent some time arranging his napkin in his lap, then sipped his wine. "It seems we're destined to remain at loggerheads."

"Destiny's overrated. That's why I carry a gun."

"In that case I suggest we make an effort to put aside our cultural differences while you're here. We're not likely to agree in any case, and it will make your stay far more pleasant for both of us."

"We need to save the unpleasantness for Bliss and Whitelaw," I said.

"Right." He tore apart a wing. "I was undecided whether to share this with you, but since we're determined to get on, here it is. There are no telegraph lines between here and the northern posts, so I depend on the monthly mail packet and the occasional long rider for news from that area. Fortunately, the service processes requests for transfer on a regular basis from troopers who find the life up there too stark for their adventurous fantasies, and these individuals carry messages from their former posts. One of them stopped here yesterday from Fort Chipewyan, up on Lake Athabasca."

I watched him nibbling at the bone in his hands. He managed to do it without getting grease in his moustache.

"The fort sends out patrols in a two-hundred-mile loop around the lake," he went on. "For supplies and information the patrols stop regularly at a trading post on the Methye Portage. The day this trooper left Chipewyan, a rider came in from the patrol with word that the trading post was in ashes. They found a burned body, which may or may not belong to the trader, a Métis named Jean-Baptiste Coupe-Jarret. That's Cutthroat in English. Colorful chap, rode with Louis Riel in the uprising in '69."

"Witnesses?"

He shook his head, deposited the bone on his plate, and used his finger bowl. "Beastly place, Methye: solid cliff with the Athabasca River boiling round it like Saturday night in Piccadilly. Only reason the post is there at all is to do business with

Indians and voyageurs carrying their canoes around the cataracts. If anyone saw anything he's down the river and gone. Only damn fools and Mounties mind anyone's business but their own in that wild country."

"It has Bliss and Whitelaw's signature."

"It could just as well have been Cree, or those Sioux from the stronghold, or those rum Métis. The Canadian Pacific has got them all stirred up this year."

"You said Coupe-Jarret was a Métis."

"He ain't the loyalist he was a dozen years ago. There's some as say he never was, and claim he sold out Riel at Fort Garry. I do know he's one of them we've depended upon for information about what the half-breeds are up to. *Coupe de poignard,* I've heard them call him: Backstabber. If he's dead, I hope they buried him deep. Otherwise the blighters will dig him up and feed him piece by piece to their ugly dogs." He bit into a breast.

"How soon do you expect details?"

"Mail packet's due any day. If it's an uprising, Chipewyan will send to Fort Vermilion for reinforcements and notify Ottawa through here. If it's your marauders, they'll handle it themselves and report. Three hundred troopers ought to be more than enough to cane a ragtag bunch of American bandits."

In the interest of putting aside our cultural differences I held my tongue. I looked at the directions again, returned them to the envelope, and put it inside my shirt. "I'll ride out tomorrow and talk to your survivor," I said. "You didn't tell me her name."

"Weathersill. Her Christian name is Hope, if you can believe it."

"I wouldn't want to know a set of parents who would name their daughter Despair."

"Yes," he said, and remembered his wine. "Quite. Perhaps I shall have good news for you when you return. You may be back in Helena in time to celebrate George Washington's birthday. Gala event, I suppose: Fireworks and pageants and the mayor parading about in tights and a powdered wig."

"No, we generally save that for Independence Day, when we beat the tights off King George." I paid for my meal, excavated my bearskin from under the coats that had accumulated on top of it, and went out, leaving George Washington face up on the table.

10

A pair of large charred log timbers formed a rude cross at the top of a mound of freshly turned earth overlooking the roiling Saskatchewan, visible for a mile through gaps in the tall pines. It marked the mass grave where Inspector Vivian and his volunteers had buried the victims of the Christmas massacre, and if it weren't for that feature I might have been a week finding the remains of the settlement; for reasons roughly having to do with the banishment from Eden, God never places gold in the middle of a well-traveled road.

However, the inspector's directions were accurate. Late in the forenoon of the second day out of Moose Jaw I pushed the mustang and pulled the gray up a hill covered with sugary snow and looked down from the top upon the black and broken evidence of atrocity.

Snow had fallen since the event, but not enough to cover the raw wound. Piles of scorched logs lay in regular patterns, spaced evenly apart like the shacks and cabins that had preceded them, with stone chimneys rising obstinately from the rubble. Some of the logs had burned entirely but retained their original shape even though they were made completely of ash and would crumble apart at the touch, like cigars left to burn themselves out forgotten in an ashtray. On the downhill side of the river opposite the settlement, a sluice built of logs sawn in half for the purpose of washing away silt and sand from recovered ore had collapsed in a broken line, its supports knocked loose with axes or kicks from horseback. After a month the scene still smelled of soot and burned flesh. I could swear I heard the echoes of gunfire, rebel yells, and the screams of the maimed, raped, and slain. Perched on that hill I felt twenty years wash away; I was back at Stone's River, after the battle.

At the near end of the string of debris appeared a white pyramid which I took at first for a snowdrift, but it turned out to be a tent made from a wagon sheet. There was no sign of life nearby. I called out that I was a friend come with supplies, and listened to my own echo bang around among the trees and ridges for the better part of a minute. When no reply came after the second time, I transferred the Winchester from its scabbard to my lap and picked my way down the grade.

The sorrel became skittish and the gray tried to back up when we reached level ground; the stench of death was faint but unmistakable. I used my spurs and jerked the lead, but after another fifty yards the gray set its feet and would not budge. I stepped down, dallied the lead around the saddle horn, and hitched the sorrel to a low spruce, then approached the tent carrying the Winchester. There was no sign of a recent campfire outside the tent, and no smoke-hole in the canvas to accommodate one inside Indian fashion. I was cold enough in my bearskin, and I had been moving. How a person managed to stick in one place in that frozen country without a fire and avoid freezing to death was a mystery. Perhaps she had died, and been dragged away by wolves or a bear. Camping the night before, I had heard the weird baby-cry of a grizzly not far away, and had built my fire large to keep from waking up with a leg gnawed off. What Bliss and Whitelaw had started, the Canadian woods might have finished.

In front of the tent I stopped and called out again. When no one answered I pulled aside the flap, sidestepping quickly in case lead came out. It didn't. I ducked my head and went inside.

What light there was came filtered through canvas. The sun was dazzling on the snow outside, and I waited a minute for my eyes to catch up to the change. Otherwise I would have been out in thirty seconds. I was alone in the tent with a buffalo-plaid blanket someone had been using for a bed and an iron-bound trunk with the lid thrown back.

Out of curiosity I stepped over and poked through the contents with the barrel of the Winchester. The trunk was full of tangled cloth, patching and dress and curtain material selected with care by a woman determined to make a civilized life for herself and her family in the wilderness. There was calico and denim and tightly woven wool, flannel and duck canvas and one slim roll of damask, expensive to obtain and wrapped in cheap blue cotton to protect it from handling. Everything else looked as if it had been pawed through recently. Some of the material was brown at the edges — part of the trunk's lid was scorched — and there was a strong smell of stale smoke, but the trunk must have been stored somewhere the flames hadn't reached. I used the carbine's muzzle to work the top off a straw sewing basket. It contained spools of gaily colored silk and cotton thread, a sheaf of dress patterns on tissue carefully folded and tied with a pink ribbon, and a handful of shriveled black walnuts stashed by a squirrel.

Two large scraps of gingham and gauzy lace were spread out side by side on the earthen floor. A pair of shears with black enameled handles and sawtooth blades lay on the gingham, freckled slightly with rust. Bits of brownish fabric lay nearby, curled like dead centipedes. Someone had been busy trimming the smoke-stained edges.

I withdrew the Winchester from the trunk, hoping I hadn't gotten any oil on the fabric. Out there among the wolves and Indians I felt as if I had violated the sanctity of a woman's bedroom. I slunk out — and that's when someone shot me and ruined billiards forever for Page Murdock.

PART TWO

Runners in the Woods

11

I've had forty years to sort things out and I still can't swear to how much of what I witnessed next actually happened and how much I dreamed through a haze of pain so thick it could almost be called a form of sleep.

Start with the shot.

The evidence of all that domestic activity involving the scraps of material in the tent had knocked the edge off the caution I normally carried into open territory along with my weapons and provisions. I threw the flap wide and stepped right out into the open with the Winchester dangling at the end of one arm. The sunlight was brilliant after the dimness inside. I saw a purple shadow against the sky and my hands were just receiving the signal to raise the carbine when something struck my right side with the force of a boulder and my feet went out from under me and I went down hard on my tailbone. My lungs collapsed and a lightning-bolt of pure white pain shot up the base of my spine to the top of my skull. I have a clear memory of realizing what had happened to me, of the importance of finding my legs and scrambling for some kind of cover before a second shot came, and then a red-and-black wash took away my sight and I teetered over backward into a hole I hadn't noticed before and fell into warm darkness. It was like tumbling back into the womb.

The rest is a tangle. I remember a woman with her hair loose and blowing wild; Farmer Donalbain's weathered features ringed by his Quaker beard; an Indian with a platinum watch chain strung across his middle just the way the meat millionaires wore them in Chicago; striped and solid-color ivory balls rolling on green baize; John Swingtree's hairless skin plastered to his skull, his body in chains; the smell of uncured buckskin boiled in some solution made of pure stench; Sloan McInerney telling Judge Blackthorne he'd spent eight hundred dollars on a cigar at the Coliseum; the sound of bone utensils clanking against each other like hollow metal; a clear tenor voice chanting, "Sharp be the blade and sure the blow and short the pang to undergo"; the taste of something warm and liquid with a greasy base and dried greens floating in it. I'm pretty sure now the chant and the ivory balls and Sloan McInerney were left over from before, and I doubt either Swingtree or Donalbain had shaken loose from their respective prisons — the territorial house in Deer Lodge and the lonely wheat farm below the Canadian border — and traveled north, but I'm undecided whether I actually saw the Cree chief Piapot, particularly since he made a strong enough impression to visit me in my dreams as recently as two months ago.

The rawhide and foul stench were real enough. When I awoke for certain and pulled aside my bear coat, which someone had spread over me like a blanket, my shirt was open and the lower half of my trunk was encased in a buckskin wrap from which all the hair had been scraped and which had dried as hard as plaster. I rapped it with my knuckles, testing it, and got a crisp report as if I'd knocked on a door. It was as tight as a corset and restricted my breathing, but I wasn't in pain. I had seen Indians repair shattered buttstocks and splintered lodge poles with the same device, but this was my first experience with it in healing.

Sunlight filtered through canvas. I was lying on the buffalo-plaid blanket I had seen before, and when I turned my head the trunk full of fabric was still there, but with the lid shut. I spotted, perched on the ground beside the blanket, a white china bowl with a delicate scalloped design around its lip, marred by a black stain and a crack on one side. I smelled cooking grease and boiled greens, and something clawed at my stomach lining. I was famished. I reached over and touched the bowl. It was still warm. I twisted a little to get both hands around it.

That was a mistake.

Pain lanced my left side. I gasped, dropped the bowl, and fell back while a sheet of white fire swept over me. Someone groaned loudly in the cracked, froggy voice of an old woman. It was me.

Something tore aside the tent flap then, allowing a brass beam of pure sunlight inside and in its middle the same purple shadow I had seen just before the door slammed in my face. I saw a glint off gun metal. I put my hands on the ground and tried to slide backward, like a startled snake slithering for cover in the shadow of a rock. The pain rocketed up my side, paralyzing my right arm. It buckled and I fell

126

over sideways, into a fresh country of pain.

I had been shot before, and taken blows, fallen off horses and trains and mountains; broken bones and been bunged up for weeks. The agony I had known those times was something I prayed to get back to from where I was now. On none of those occasions had I been hurt so badly I didn't care if someone put a bullet in my brain. I peered through the throbbing watery fog at a woman with her hair loose and blowing wild, at the great gaping muzzle of the horse pistol she had pointed at me, and didn't care which end she used on me as long as it put me back in that warm dark womb I'd had the bad sense to crawl out of in the first place.

The pain reached high tide and began to recede. My vision cleared, particle by particle, like bubbles bursting. The woman was a giant, standing over me with her shoulders hunched slightly to keep her head from brushing the top of the tent; but then I remembered I had had to stoop as well the first time I entered it, and that now I was looking up from the ground. She wore a man's canvas coat that hung loosely enough to expose the blanket lining, the cuffs turned back a couple of times, but apart from that she was dressed as a woman, in a plain brown dress whose hem hung to the insteps of her lace-up boots, its edge dirty and tattered from dragging the ground. She had a cartridge belt buckled around her waist with six inches of leather flapping free because she'd had to punch an extra hole to make it fit and an empty holster. The revolver that belonged to the holster, a huge Walker Colt designed for carriage in a scabbard attached to a saddle, was heavy enough to bend her wrist with its weight, but she didn't look as if she wanted to put it down any time soon. Her other hand was occupied with a double-barreled Stevens ten-gauge shotgun, the kind Wells Fargo messengers carried, with the muzzles pointed at the ground. I counted myself fortunate that when the time had come to shoot me she had decided to use the pistol. If it had been the shotgun there wouldn't have been enough left of me to shovel into the tent.

She had a good face, if you liked strong bones and eyes that didn't shift. The skin was sunburned from the light reflecting strong off the snow, peeling like old paint, but with a good scrubbing and some powder and rouge, it would turn the occasional male head at even so jaded a place as Delmonico's in New York. Just now it was severe and hawklike, the pale gray eyes as hard as January ice and just about as responsive. There was an animal alertness in them but no sign of human intelligence.

"I'm guessing you're Mrs. Weathersill." My voice scarcely qualified as a croak. "My name's Murdock. I came from Moose Jaw with provisions."

Hope Weathersill — for it could have been no other — said nothing, and gave no indication that she'd understood my words. After a long time her eyes moved, flicking toward the spilled bowl next to the blanket, then back to me quickly, as if I might make an attempt of some kind while her gaze was elsewhere. After another long silence she moved, and at the end of so much stillness it was as if the Cascade Range had lifted its skirts and danced the Virginia reel. However, all she did was insert the muzzles of her shotgun inside the bowl, slide it over toward herself, and stoop to pick it up, during which her eyes and the Colt remained on me. When she had the bowl in the same hand in which she held the shotgun, she backed out of the tent. Through the open flap I saw an edge of yellow flame and heard wood crackling. She returned without the shotgun, but still held the big revolver in one hand with the bowl steaming in the other. The bowl must have been hot to the touch, but as she holstered the Colt and shifted the bowl to that hand I saw that her palms were shiny with callus; the life out there had been hard long before the massacre, and she would have taken her turn chopping wood and driving the mules and horses to pull up stumps. Beyond that her hands, face, and dress were smudged with soot. There was soot in her hair as well, and it was tangled and snarled so badly it would have been easier to cut than comb. Only that delicate bowl and, when she knelt beside me and shipped soup into a spoon, the ornate filigreed silver of the handle between her thumb and forefinger bore witness to more civilized aspirations, clouded now by green tarnish.

Painfully I propped myself up on one elbow to accept the spoon between my lips. She made no attempt to support my head, although as a wife and mother, she would have been skilled in the details of tending to the injured and ill; as a widow with slain children, she knew that I could not attack her easily as long as I needed one arm to keep from sprawling onto my back.

The soup tasted better than I remembered from my delirium — less greasy, the greens richer and more full-bodied. Her eyes — close up, they had a yellow-amber tint, like those of a wild creature encountered unexpectedly — never left me as she worked the spoon. She might have been nursing a wounded predator, keeping it alive for reasons of her own without trust or tenderness.

"The supplies are on the gray pack horse I brought," I said between swallows. "I was riding a mustang. I hope you're taking as good care of them as you are of me."

She filled the spoon again and brought it to my lips. There was no sign that she understood.

When the bowl was empty she rose and backed out of the tent once again. Alone and still supported on my elbow, I inspected the stiff rawhide wrap. It was Indian work, I was sure. What I wasn't so sure of was whether Piapot had had a hand in it or if I had dreamt his presence. If he had, I was at a loss to explain why he should care whether I survived. The Indians I had known respected a man with sand in his belly, if that was what I had shown during our parley, but in time of conflict they were not so beguiled by it they went out of their way to restore life to a man who might bring that sand to bear against them another day. Maybe the Indians in Canada were different. Certainly the Mounties had a lower casualty record in their dealings with the northern tribes than had the American cavalry on the high plains. Given that, what influence they had with the feral thing that had been Hope Weathersill was a mystery. They revered — or feared — human madness, but the mad did not generally return the favor. The whole damn country was upside-down.

I probed my left side gently through the wrap. A sharp stab answered, but I forced myself to continue exploring until I was satisfied as to the extent of the damage. I had two or three cracked ribs anyway, but I was pretty sure there wasn't a bullet in there. Either the woman had grazed me with the big Colt or the bearskin had stopped or deflected the bullet so that I took only its impact and wasn't punctured. But the impact of a two-hundred-grain ball of lead traveling at the rate of 410 feet per second is nothing to ignore; a six-hundred-pound log rolling off the back of a lumber wagon couldn't hit harder or make a bigger bruise. The entire side was tender, and since I couldn't inhale deeply enough to fill both lungs because of how tightly I was constricted I wasn't sure that one of them hadn't collapsed.

I felt my head getting light and lay back. Now I saw there was much less room in the tent than when I had first entered it. I recognized some of the bags of flour and the huge salt pork I had brought out from town for Inspector Vivian stacked to one side. It was a heavy load for one woman to carry. The Indians had probably helped, either for a percentage of the goods or because they felt sorry for the madwoman living alone in the wilderness — or just because they were Indians and made a point of bizarre behavior. On that thought I drifted off. I dreamed I was in Helena, dealing myself a hand of patience on the rickety table next to the Detroit stove in the house I rented in town and getting up from time to time to turn the trout I had frying in my old skillet, covered in corn-flour batter and swimming in hot butter. With the part of me that was still alert I thought that if I could keep that dream going long enough I'd wake up into it from the reality I was living.

12

When I awoke again, night had fallen. I didn't know which night it was, or how many I had slept through or ignored in my delirium. The fire was still burning outside, casting rippling shadows through the canvas.

The frozen earth beneath me was as stiff as hardrock maple and made me ache in a hundred places where my body curved and it didn't. My bladder was full to the point of agony. But I was reluctant to try to get up because I knew a universe of pain was hovering just above me, waiting for me to stir from the safe haven beneath. I was forty years old, if the faded brown ink on the end pages of the Bible that had come over from Scotland with my father meant anything, and had faced more punishment than most adventurous men twice my age, but the older I got, the more it hurt, and the less prepared I was to suffer it. I was going to be a cowardly old man.

I rolled over slowly, out from under the

bearskin cover, stopped to breathe, placed my palms flat against the earth, took in as much breath as I could hold, and pushed myself up onto my knees. A wave of thick gluey fog rolled in, gray and glistening. My eyesight started to go. I caught it when it was reduced to pinpoints of light and forced them open by sheer force of will and a lifetime's experience of blackouts; when you've lived through the same nightmare a score of times you learn to recognize it and exercise some control over it. My elbows wanted to buckle, I wobbled. The wave passed on through the other side of my skull. I remained motionless on my hands and knees until I was sure it was all out. Then I shoved myself upright and let the momentum carry me off my knees and onto my feet. I did this all in one movement, like ripping off a bandage. Getting the worst part out of the way all at once.

The worst was worse than I thought. The wave reversed itself in a towering curl, blocking out the light. I grabbed for the tent pole with both hands, felt the coarse bark, and tightened my grip, imprinting the whorls and ridges on my palms. The inside of the curl was lined with hot orange pain. It was like getting shot all over again. I increased my grip on the pole, tried to crush the straight pine, to make my hands hurt worse than what was going on around the middle of my body. The wave crested, hung frozen for a week, then ducked its head and went on over. I hung on to the pole and rode it out. The burning slid down from my trunk to my pelvis and down my legs and out the ends of my toes. I stood shaking in the aftermath.

When I thought I could support myself I took one hand away, then the other. Some of the bark came off with them. My fingernails were bleeding. They throbbed when I fumbled the bone buttons of my shirt through the eyelets. One side of my body, the side opposite the fire burning outside the tent, was cold. I looked down at the bearskin, lying at my feet, as far away as Helena. I didn't dare bend down and try to pick it up. I didn't have enough left to make that trip all over again.

I pulled aside the flap and stepped outside, hugging myself to keep the heat in. The sky was clear of clouds, allowing outer space to come clear to the ground, black as a bottomless well and studded with stars like ice crystals. The air was searingly cold; breathing it in was like plunging chest deep into an icy creek. A fresh fall of snow, over now, covered the raw broken edges of the ruined settlement and gentled the steep slope to the river, chuckling away between the jagged wafers of ice that lined its banks. The place looked as it might have before civilization had stretched out its left arm and closed its fingers around it.

Hope Weathersill sat cross-legged in the snow twenty feet from the tent, on the far edge of the firelight. Her back was turned my way, but she must have heard me, because the snow squeaked like sprung planks beneath my boots. She didn't turn around or stir as I approached the fire. It had begun to burn down. I spotted a pile of limbs nearby, powdered with snow. I went over, bent my knees to keep from stooping, slid one off the pile, shook off the snow, and dragged it over to the fire, where I dropped the end into the flames. Breaking it up would have damaged me worse than the limb. I saw the other end had been chopped with an axe or a tomahawk; either the pile was left over from Vivian's last visit or the Indians were helping out.

A spluttering snort drew my attention to the horses. The sorrel mustang and the woolly gray were standing a hundred feet closer to the tent than the spot where I had hitched them. I walked that way. They were hobbled with braided rawhide thongs and someone had unsaddled them and unfolded their saddle blankets and spread them over their backs for warmth. I found the saddles themselves close by, stacked and covered with the canvas wrap from my bedroll, sifted over with snow. The bag of oats was there as well and I fed two handfuls apiece to the horses, who accepted them greedily as if they hadn't eaten in days. But whoever had relieved them of their burdens and bothered to cover the saddles would have taken care to feed them as well. I assumed the bedroll and my pouches were also underneath the cover but I didn't investigate that far because I felt myself getting weak.

The fire was going well now. I stopped next to it to warm my hands and draw the chill out of my bones, then approached the woman, once again making plenty of noise to avoid startling her. She didn't move. Her back was so straight and she was so still sitting there in just the canvas coat with her head uncovered that I had a bad feeling even before I circled around to face her. Her eyes were open. There was frost in her eyebrows and bits of ice in her wild hair. The shotgun lay across her lap with her hands resting on it, the fingers as blue as bottle necks. I took in air, held it against the pain in my ribs, then let it out in a thick plume and bent my knees to see if there was any vapor at all coming from her nose or mouth.

The shotgun came up fast and struck me along my right jawline with a noise as if a great iron bell had rung inside my head. I lost my balance and fell backward into the snow, which wasn't as soft as it needed to be for a man who didn't take pain as well as he used to. The wave came back, all bright orange now and no longer thick or sluggish. When it subsided, dragging its flotsam of razor-sharp needles, I found myself staring up both barrels of the shotgun. The woman was standing over me once again, with the wildness in her eyes and her hair blowing about like smoke. Both hammers were back and her finger rested on the front trigger.

The only thing I was thinking was what a shame the Indians had wasted all that time wrapping my ribs, just to get shot again and for keeps.

Her expression — it was no expression at all, comes to that — didn't change. She lowered each hammer in turn, using her thumbs, then poked me in the chest with the muzzles. When I didn't react she poked me again, hard enough to awaken the pain. I got the meaning then and gripped the barrels with both hands, feeling them weld themselves to the metal in the cold. I drew up one knee and she braced herself and leaned back, hauling me to my feet with the shotgun as a lever. I hoped neither of the hammers was loose and the powder in the shells was stable, because the muzzles were pointed at my midsection the whole time.

Then I was on my feet and she snatched away the gun, taking some of the skin of my palms along with it, and returned to the hollow in the snow where she had been sitting. In another second she was back in position with the shotgun across her lap with hands resting on it and her eyes wide open, breathing so shallowly she made almost no steam. I followed the line of her gaze to the charred timber of the cross overlooking the mass grave on the ridge, where her husband and children were lying in a jumble with the rest of the massacred, joined for eternity.

I waited with her for a little, then I got cold. I went back to the fire and stood with my back to the flames to dry my clothes. When that was done I dragged another two feet of unburned limb into the fire and returned to the tent, where I picked up my dream where I had left off, my first lucky break of the trip.

When morning came around — the next one or the one after that; it's been too long and at the time the passage of hours and days held no significance — I knew I was getting better because my brain had begun to go bad from boredom. I was slept out. The soup, which never seemed to run dry, had lost all taste, and I only tolerated it because the feeding sessions broke up the day. For a time I amused myself wondering why the Weathersill woman bothered. That stopped interesting me when I decided it gave her something to do aside from sitting and staring. She had me down as the enemy, but she had spent too much of her life taking care of someone to resist the habit. She didn't give this any more thought than one of those birds that continue to care for strange hatchlings long after they were aware that the eggs had been left in their nests by a trespasser. Everything she did came from instinct, like breathing. Bliss and Whitelaw had gutted her as effectively as their torches had the buildings of the settlement.

Or perhaps not. For all I knew she spent her silent hours thinking up recipes for when the soup finally ran out or composing speeches for the Grand Army of the Republic. Assuming too much was what got lawmen shot.

When I sat up this particular morning, the pain had backed off to the extent that I welcomed it as a troublesome friend whose visits gave structure to one's life. I stood, caught my breath when one of my cracked ribs pinched my side, but prevented myself from grasping the tent pole. I found my balance without it and even worked up courage to lift the bearskin and slide it over my shoulders cloak fashion. I had trained myself to take shallow breaths and make them satisfy. I stroked my matted beard, attempting to reckon the time I'd been there by the length of the whiskers; but if I were good at arithmetic I wouldn't have agreed to the salary I was being paid.

I went out — and blinked at the sight of a thousand bright-red tunics facing the tent in a semicircle on horseback. It was more color than I'd seen since the leaves fell in autumn.

13

Behold the prodigal," Inspector Vivian said. "Except his father didn't have to go looking for him."

He was seated astride a tall chestnut so dark it could have passed for a black in slight shadow, curried to a high gloss like burnished leather. He held the reins in one gauntleted hand while the other rested on his thigh. Only a career British cavalryman could have looked so uncomfortable in the saddle. He was dressed, like the others, in heavy scarlet wool, with a belt making a diagonal white slash across his torso and a white cork helmet with a spike on top and the strap buckled tight to his chin. The red-white combination put me in mind of strawberries and cream.

There weren't really a thousand of them, of course. The actual number was closer to fifty, but the effect of that crimson band separating white earth from blue sky inflated the initial estimate. I understood then the reason behind the color choice in

London; no matter what the size of your own force, you couldn't look at it without feeling outnumbered.

In the middle ground between the semicircle and the tent, Hope Weathersill sat Indian fashion in her usual spot, still as a plaster Buddha. The great armed body of men didn't exist for her. She saw straight through it to the cross on the ridge.

I slid my gaze from one end of the line to the other and back to Vivian. "All for me?"

"Yes, they are debating your predicament on the floor of Parliament. Gladstone himself took up your case. We are here on his orders to escort you to Balmoral, where you will be knighted by Her Majesty. Moose Jaw Murdock, they shall call you in the *Times*. Like Chinese Gordon."

"She'll have to come here. I get seasick."

His sense of humor had reached its shallow bottom. "When you hadn't returned after five days I decided to look in on you on our way north. These men have been dispatched from Fort Walsh and placed under my command. This expedition is bound for Fort Chipewyan."

I had to pry my brain loose from where it had been stuck for days to recall our conversation in the Prince of Wales. I remembered the dead trader on the

144

Methye Portage. "On your way to avenge John Cutthroat?"

"Not entirely. The mail packet I was expecting from Chipewyan arrived the day after you left. It contained a general requisition for reinforcements from throughout the Dominion. The commander up there believes the same band that killed Jean-Baptiste Coup-Jarret and burned his post are responsible for the slaughter of a Métis family living on the south shore of Lake Athabasca, directly across from the fort. With the Métis situation as it is, the government in Ottawa is granting the request for reinforcements to prevent civil war."

I felt my strength returning. It started as a tingling sensation at the base of my neck and shot through my body in a flash of heat. "Survivors?"

"One, briefly. A boy of about ten. Before he died he provided a description of the men he saw assaulting his mother after they shot him in the chest, evidently to weaken her resistance. Two of them match the readers your Judge Blackthorne sent on Lorenzo Bliss and Charles Whitelaw."

"I'll get my gear together." I started toward the canvas covering my saddles and pouches.

"You'll slow us down. What happened to you, by the way?" He might have been asking about a holiday in Scotland.

I found the Winchester carbine and Evans rifle under the cover, also the Deane-Adams with my cartridge belt neatly wrapped around the holster. Whatever medicine a crazy woman carried, it must have been plenty powerful to prevent the Indians from confiscating good weapons.

"Let's just say I got a little more out of the Weathersill woman than I came for." I buckled on the belt.

He turned his pale eyes on the woman. "I'm half surprised she didn't make an end to the job once she'd started."

"Only half?"

"I doubt even Canada could blow all the female out of her. Or out of any woman, for that matter. I suppose it was she who patched you up."

"No, I have your renegade chief to thank for that."

"Piapot? That old rotter! You must have made quite an impression on him." He gathered his reins. "When you get back to Moose Jaw, ask for Bernard Eel. He ain't a doctor, but he put in a year as a dresser at St. Bart before he lost his place; something about theft. He's the closest thing to a medical professional in this damned part of the country."

I checked the load in the Deane-Adams. "I'm not going back to Moose Jaw."

"Go where you like, so long as it ain't with us. I'm not in the habit of carrying wounded *into* battle."

"A few days ago you told me three hundred Mounties ought to be more than enough to handle Bliss and Whitelaw. One battered American lawman more or less shouldn't make any difference."

"Ottawa doesn't agree. When a general order goes out, it's to be obeyed yesterday. We're not waiting round while you get saddled. Sergeant Major?"

A pair of black moustaches with a sunburned face behind them stood in his stirrups and bawled something incomprehensible, at least to me. The line of men turned their horses north in a single graceful movement, as easily as a man swinging one arm.

I had to raise my voice above the jingling of bit-chains. "When you see you're being followed, do me a favor and don't shoot."

"It won't be a favor when you lose the trail in a great bloody blizzard," he called back. "I smell one coming."

"Where can I find a guide?"

"Moose Jaw."

If I'd been any longer outfitting the sorrel and getting the pack saddle and the supplies and provisions I needed onto the gray, the Canadian Pacific would have finished laying its tracks, and I might have ridden to Fort Chipewyan in a Pullman. I had to rest often to keep my ribs from poking out my side, and when the damn mustang puffed its belly to prevent me from tightening the cinch I had to wait until it couldn't hold its wind any more, then yank fast; kicking the animal in the gut wasn't an option in my condition. Finally I cut the hobbles, found my badger hat, and stepped into leather with the help of a pile of half-burned logs to start from. I snicked my way over to where the woman was seated. Her hands, red and chapped with black ragged nails, dangled between her spread thighs, and the only movement was her hair crawling in the gusts and the faint gray jets of smoke her breath made when I leaned out from the saddle to see it. She neither blinked nor moved her eyes from the cross on the ridge. I couldn't tell if she was aware of the Mounties' visit or if she cared. To this day I don't know whether her method of living was a form of surrender or a determination to survive; or if the enormity of the catastrophe that had befallen her had reduced her to the level of a machine, which continued to operate long after those who had depended on it no longer had a use for it. If that was the case, I wondered how long it would go on. I couldn't tell if the assistance she received from the Indians and Vivian was a kindness or a despicable evil, sentencing her to a lifetime of bleak vigilance at the grave of those she loved when it would be more merciful to let her perish. Whatever the situation, I have only to sit back with nothing occupying my thoughts to see her again as clearly as if I were still in that ruined settlement; watching, always watching.

I turned the mustang's head, jerked the pack line, and left her there.

I had no intention of going back to Moose Jaw. I'd brought enough provisions beyond those I'd left for the woman to see me through several more days on the road. If I could follow the Mounties' trail as far as the next settlement or lumber camp, where I could trade for more or at least hire a guide, I stood as good a chance of survival as came to a peace officer west of St. Louis and north of God. Game was plentiful, according to the rabbit and deer tracks and great cowlike prints left by elk that crisscrossed the trail. I wouldn't starve, although I'd miss the coffee when it ran out.

Vivian was right about snow coming. I'd grown up in mountain country, recognized that bitter-iron smell, and felt a fresh ache in my damaged ribs and in an old bullet wound I'd forgotten except when the weather was about to change sharply. I calculated I had about twenty-four hours before it came in hard enough to obliterate the trail and picked up my pace. The hide wrap was acutely uncomfortable in the saddle, but as it kept the cracked bones from shaking the rest of the way apart on the trot I was happy I had it.

I'd brought a map of western Canada I'd acquired in Helena, full of blank spots and scratchy lines that might have been rivers or marks made by hairs stuck to the cartographer's pen. Nearing dark I heard water chuckling and decided I'd reached the north fork of the Saskatchewan River. There was a Mountie post in that area, Battleford, where Vivian's men would likely put in for the night, but I could no longer see the trail. The energy I'd have to spend looking for it was better invested crossing the river; fordable streams had a way of becoming torrents overnight, adding days or weeks to a journey in the search for a place to cross. I had just enough light to pick my way among the rocks visible in the shallow bed, kneeing the reluctant sorrel and jerking at the lead line when the gray balked at the icy water coursing past its fetlocks. Once on the opposite bank I dismounted quickly and built a fire with pine needles and boughs for the horses to thaw their numb legs. The air was bitter cold, and not cold enough; not far enough below zero anyway to prevent snow from forming. I smelled the air and changed my mind about my earlier estimate. The flakes would be falling by dawn.

I fed the horses, cooked bacon and beans in the skillet, washed them down with coffee, and wrapped myself in my furs and blanket, drawing down the badger hat until it touched my collar and leaving no skin exposed. Sometime during the night I heard the wind starting, whistling through distant pines and coming my way with the speed of a late freight racing to make up time on the downgrade. By the time it got to the branches overhead it was howling. I got up to feed the fire and ran right into the gray. Both horses had moved in close, rumps to the wind. I stroked and patted them to assure them I had things under control and bundled myself up again to sleep the sleep of the innocent. There's no sin in lying to a horse.

I heard the first grainy flakes pelting my furs, then slid off into senselessness. When gray light woke me, the furs felt as if they weighed a hundred pounds. I raised my head and a shelf of snow avalanched down my neck, chilling me to the base of my spine. When I looked down, my body had disappeared. In its place was a white tent. I was a human snowdrift.

Pushing myself to my feet required both hands. It was like sliding out from under a cloak of lead. The stuff was still falling, if falling was the word; the wind hooted and the snow came in sideways, stinging my face like flung pebbles. I leaned into it, snapping my eyes open at intervals to see where I was going, then squeezing them shut, full of water, to keep the snow out. The fire had gone out long since, suffocated beneath a thick wet blanket.

The horses were huddled together for warmth. Snow clung to their coats and masks of hoarfrost encased their faces, made of their frozen breath with their eyes looking pitiably through the holes. I used the Deane-Adams to break up the ice, fed them each a handful of grain to start their blood flowing, shook the snow off my gear, and led them to the shelter of a tight stand of pines farther up the slope from the river. The snow was nearly waist high where the ground dished in. Inside the stand, where the trunks grew so close they made a sort of rick and acted as a drift fence, the earth was almost bare. I strapped on the horses' nose bags, opened a can of sardines with my knife, and sat down in a cradle formed by forked trunks to eat and wait out the worst of the storm. I couldn't build a fire for fear of loosening the snow in the tree-tops and creating a slide that would bury us all.

The blizzard broke shortly before noon. The last gunmetal-colored cloud slid across a hole in the trees like a window shade going up, exposing bright blue sky. The wind leveled off, then quit abruptly. The silence hurt my ears. When I stepped outside the pines, into a horseshoe of ankle-high snow left by the passage of wind around the dense stand, surrounded by towering drifts, the geography had changed completely from the night before. From one horizon to the other stretched a dazzling clean sheet of white. Even the trees were mere shadows beneath heavy clumps that bent them nearly to the ground, as if the wind together with the flinty abrasive grains had planed the landscape clear of everything vertical except the mountains, which stood impossibly high and aloof to heaven and earth. Sunlight walloped off the brutal white, blinding me like a photographer's magnesium flash. I was looking out at a white desert.

The trail I had been following was gone, utterly and forever. I went back, blacked my eyes from the can of lampblack, mounted the mustang, and led the gray out of the trees. The little sorrel had to raise its legs to its belly to gain leverage against the drifts. I rode it down the slope to the river and turned west. If there was a guide to be found who could lead me to Fort Chipewyan, I would find him near water. Failing that, I stood a better chance of having my remains discovered on the bank come the thaw than if I ventured across the vast blankness to the north. I couldn't have Judge Blackthorne thinking I'd welshed on our bet and deserted.

14

Fils de la catin!"

The words, delivered in a loud, phlegmy baritone, carried a long way. I heard them, and those that followed, twenty minutes before I saw the cabin, a low dugout affair, built along the lines of a railroad car, with its roof heaped with snow. French was not my long suit, but I had heard enough of it during my travels in a frontier made up of expatriates from around the world to figure out, with the help of the vicious flood of language that came after, that someone or something was being called a son of a bitch.

As I drew near I made out the figure of a man standing atop what appeared to be a stack of corrugated-iron sheets at the end of the cabin, sunk up to his knees in snow and using a shovel to scoop the heavy white stuff off the surface and onto the ground eight feet below. The underarm movement was what I first noticed, because the heavy capote the man was

155

wearing was the exact blue of the sky behind him. The hood was flung back to expose a fall of curly black hair to his shoulders and the glint of a piratical gold hoop in the lobe of his left ear. His diatribe, punctuated with grunts and short exhalations that issued from his mouth in bright silver jets, continued unabated as I came to the edge of the shadow the cabin threw in the late afternoon sun; I couldn't tell if he even knew I was there.

I was close enough then to realize he wasn't standing on iron sheets. My nose told me they were green buffalo hides, stiff with frozen gore. The mercury would have to go down a lot more to stop them from stinking.

"Merde!"

This last remark was accompanied by a flash of bright metal as the shovel skidded out of his hands, executed a somersault in the air, and knifed down blade first straight at me. I yanked the reins left, the sorrel leapt sideways, stumbling. Instinctively I leaned right to keep it from falling over left. This put me back in the path of the flying shovel, which glanced off my shoulder, ripping a long gash in the bearskin, and chunked solidly into the snow with the handle twanging. The pain arced around to my left side, just in time to connect with the one coming from my ribs. My whole body went into shock, but I managed to jerk the Evans rifle from its scabbard and point it at the man standing atop the hides.

"Non!" He spread his arms, showing his open palms. There was English mixed in with the flood of French that followed, but it came too fast for me to make it out. His tone said he was explaining or apologizing or both.

I didn't shoot him. He wasn't armed, and with the pain coursing through my body the effort of squeezing the trigger sounded like no fun. I let the hammer down gently.

"You are not injured, *monsieur,* no?" He lowered his arms.

"I am injured, yes," I said. "Climb down off those stinking skins."

He had the agility of a monkey. A narrow lodgepole stripped of its bark stood at each corner of the stack of hides and he gripped one in both hands and slid down slick as grease. I saw then that the poles had been erected to support a flat roof made of shakes to shelter the hides and that it had collapsed under the weight of the snow. He had been standing on what remained of the roof, shoveling it clear.

The little man — his chin came just above my knee where I sat aboard the mustang — saw that I was surveying the snow damage. "I am not so fine as a builder, monsieur. I am the hell of a fine hunter of the buffalo."

"I can see that." I scabbarded the Evans and probed at my shoulder through the tear in the bearskin. It was tender, but no blood came away with my hand. The blade hadn't broken the skin. "You're Métis?"

"Métis, *oui*." He lowered his eyelids. They were heavy to begin with, and along with the pencil-thin moustache that followed precisely the line of his delicately curved upper lip gave him the look of the lecherous villain in a melodrama on stage. His dusky features were more pretty than handsome. "You are Mounted Police, no?"

"I'm American. You're alone here?"

"My friends are near."

That was a lie. There wasn't another manmade structure in sight, and there was only one set of tracks between the cabin and the hide stack.

"I'm not a bandit," I said. "I'm a deputy United States marshal trailing a gang of desperadoes from Montana. Do you know the way to Fort Chipewyan?"

"I know the way. Also I know the way is long. You seek a guide, yes?"

His lids opened on the last part, light showing in his dark eyes. Buffalo butchering paid well, but it was brutal work and unless the operation was outfitted well enough to ferry the hides to civilization on a constant basis, paydays came many months apart. In guide work you got paid just to ride; and as everyone in Mexico and Canada was aware, Americans were all robber barons and rich as Vanderbilt.

I saw no reason to set him straight, but produced a leather sack containing the money I'd drawn from Judge Blackthorne for expenses. The heavy gold coins shifted and clanked when I bounced it on my palm. I tossed it at him without warning. He fumbled, then slapped it against his chest in both hands. While he was doing that I unholstered the Deane-Adams and rolled back the hammer.

"Take out a double eagle and throw the rest back. You get another one when we get to Chipewyan. Don't try to help yourself while I'm sleeping. I keep one eye open and my finger on the trigger."

He hesitated, hefting the sack. Then he shook his head and threw it back without taking a coin. I caught it one-handed —

159

barely — and studied him closely. He was dressed colorfully after the fashion of the Mètis; the capote open to expose a calico shirt and yellow buckskin leggings with a scarlet military sash knotted about his waist, fringed moccasins to his knees, but he was by no means prosperous or he wouldn't be living in a dugout with greased paper in the windows for glass and wrestling the hides off buffalo.

"I cannot, monsieur. It is ten days to Chipewyan, longer in this deep snow, and that much again to return. My wife and boy will starve." He looked ineffably sad, double eagles being scarce everywhere, and rare as jackalopes in that wild country. Then the lower half of his face broke into a gold-toothed smile. "They will not starve if they go with me."

"This is a manhunt, not a family picnic. We'll be traveling slow enough as it is."

"Fleurette rides as well as any man, and Claude can run like a rabbit and catch game with his bare hands. They will not slow us down."

"I'll keep looking. Where is the nearest settlement?"

"You'll not see another soul for two hundred miles. I am, you see, the court of last resort." The gold teeth shone.

"I don't see any horses."

"Down by the river there is a hollow in the bank with the overhang for a roof. I could not have built a better barn."

"What do they call you?"

"Philippe Louis-Napoleon Charlemagne Voltaire Murat du la Rochelle." He snapped his head forward in a bow, the hoop in his ear catching the light. "You may address me as Philippe."

"I think I'd better. Page Murdock." I leathered the pistol, drummed my fingers on my thigh, then braced myself for the pain and dismounted into the knee-deep snow. "Let's go meet the wife and child."

The inside of the cabin was surprisingly pleasant. We stepped down onto a glazed earthen floor and stood in the light from a fireplace built of river stones worn as smooth and round as forged cannonballs. The log walls were chinked expertly and hung with steelpoint engravings slit from periodicals and mounted in handmade frames. There were three split-bottom chairs, an oilcloth-covered table, a narrow bed built into one corner beneath a crucifix on the wall, and in the opposite corner a stand supporting a carved figure of the Virgin Mary with a squat tallow candle flickering in front of it.

A small woman in a plain gray dress stood on the hearth, stirring a pot suspended by chains over the flames. Her black hair was cut boyishly short, but when she turned to see who had come in, her face was as dark as any Indian's, darker than Philippe's. She had small sharp features and eyes that tilted toward her nose. Plainly she was the mother of the boy of about ten who sat on one of the chairs tying a shoe: short black hair, dusky skin, small pointed nose, and those eyes, almost Oriental and as shiny as polished obsidian. He wore a plain homespun shirt and trousers with nothing Indian about them. He showed no fear at the appearance of a stranger in his home, only quiet curiosity.

Philippe handled the introductions as if he were reading from a book of etiquette, presenting me to Fleurette and young Claude to me and repeating all our names. Fleurette, abandoning her cooking, surprised me by sinking into a quick curtsy. Claude kept his seat, studying me, until his father barked at him in French, whereupon he hopped to his feet and bowed from the waist.

"I ask you to pardon the behavior of my son, who seems determined to remain a savage." Philippe directed this at the boy with an edge in his voice.

There was nothing to say to that, so I unbuttoned my coat. It was close in the cabin. Claude raced up to take the bear-skin and stood on tiptoe to hang it on a peg by the door. I hung the badger hat on the same peg and ran my fingers through my hair. I felt disheveled in the presence of so much domesticity. But for the logs and the plain furnishings and the buffalo robe on the floor, which probably served as the youngster's bed, I might have been stand-ing in a parlor in Chicago. The place had that feel.

"You will eat with us." It was a thing set-tled, the way Philippe said it. "I hope you have no objection to squirrel."

"Thank you. I've eaten wolf and was glad I had it."

He laughed, loud and booming for a small man. "Someday I shall meet an American adventurer who has *not* eaten wolf. I begin to think you serve it at Easter. *Non, mais, non!* The head of the table." He pulled out a chair from the other side.

The table was square, and I could see no difference, but I came around and waited beside that chair while Fleurette brought the pot to the table and seated herself, her husband hastening over to hold her chair.

He took the third.

I sat, and realized all the chairs were taken. "What about Claude?"

"When there is a guest he dines later. That is a rule of this house." As he spoke he stared at Claude. The boy turned away, stood on tiptoe again to slide a book from the fireplace mantel, and sat on the edge of the bed to read. When he opened the book I saw the title: *Wuthering Heights*.

Philippe saw where I was looking. "I traded a good robe in Battleford for a valise full of books last year. Claude is learning to read. He will not be illiterate like his mother and father."

"No one's teaching him?"

"An American missionary taught him to read and write his name. He can pick out the letters. The rest will fall into place with time."

"If his name is as long as his father's, he's got most of the alphabet already."

Philippe lifted the pot and ladled a steaming heap of meat, thick gravy, and what might have been chunks of wild onion onto my tin plate. When I smelled it, I realized I hadn't eaten since sardines for breakfast. He served his wife and himself, then lowered his head and spoke quietly in French. He and his wife crossed themselves and we dug in. The squirrel was as tender as aged beef and the pungent onions tamed the gaminess. Given more genteel ingredients, Fleurette could have been head chef in any hotel in St. Louis; except as a half-breed she'd have been barred at the door.

"You will pardon me while I explain our plans to my wife," Philippe said. "She is ignorant and does not understand English."

I told him to go ahead. Carefully he put down his spoon, a wise move because he gestured with both hands when he talked. It was not all French. Although I'd heard Sioux and Cheyenne and even a little Apache down in New Mexico, I wasn't familiar with most of the tribal dialects, but the throat action is similar among Indians everywhere and I assumed he was speaking Cree part of the time, or a mix of Cree and some French dialect no self-respecting Parisian would acknowledge as stemming from his language. Her responses — some of them seemed to be questions — were more Indian than French, but she had a low silken voice that sounded pleasant even when she was plainly upset by what her husband was saying. I didn't need to speak the language to know she was in favor of staying put. I heard Claude's name frequently; she didn't like the idea of exposing her son to what fate held in store for travelers in the Canadian wilderness.

Claude, I saw, was only pretending to read *Wuthering Heights*. Whatever her charms as a novelist, Emily Brönte's windblown moors didn't stack up to a frontier manhunt in a boy's imagination.

Abruptly, with a Gallic grunt and an outward slashing motion of his hands, Philippe put an end to the discussion. He turned to me with a deep flush showing beneath his dusky pigment. "It is all arranged, *monsieur le depute*. Madame du la Rochelle and young Master Claude will be enchanted to accompany us upon our great trek north."

He flinched when Madame du la Rochelle shot to her feet, but held my gaze as she snatched away our plates and utensils, marched to the wooden tub set beside the fireplace, and dumped them inside with a clatter. I had the thought then she wasn't entirely ignorant of English.

15

Women are impossible to feature. Being the man responsible for the prospect of Fleurette and her son traveling some four hundred miles through the dead of winter from the comfort and safety of their home, I expected little in the way of welcome. Instead I was forced to conduct a fierce argument through Philippe to persuade her to let me sleep that night in my own blankets rather than surrender the bed she shared with her husband. That was the Indian side of her nature coming through, as much as the female; tribal law since before Columbus dictated that not even a mortal enemy will be denied the full hospitality of the lodge when night fell.

I awoke at first light to the smell of baking. Fleurette had biscuits baking in a Dutch oven, with coffee boiling in a blackened pot. Philippe was sitting on the edge of the bed, scratching his scalp through his spill of tightly curled hair and yawning, with his hairless legs showing between the hem of his nightshirt and the rolled tops of heavy gray woolen socks like lumbermen wore. He stood and stretched, his joints popping like small-arms fire, then stripped off the nightshirt with no concern for his nudity or who saw it. He had the muscles of an athlete, egg-shaped and fluid, and an ugly pale oblong scar just below his right shoulder blade where a bullet had been removed years before, creating as always worse damage coming out than it had going in. I made a note to ask him about it as soon as my voice woke up; discretion went out the window when it came to the past of someone you were planning to pack along through raw country.

He dressed in the same calico shirt, leggings, and moccasins he'd had on the day before, shrugged into his ankle-length capote, and headed outdoors, presumably to visit the little slant-roofed outhouse behind the cabin. On the way to the door he nudged his son awake with a toe in the ribs. Claude, still dressed, rolled out of the buffalo robe on the floor and got woozily to his feet. He was no better outfitted for morning than I. I approved of him for that. Most of the world's wickedness is done by men who go to bed with the birds and wake up sharp as fangs.

When I put on my bearskin, I saw that the gash in the shoulder was repaired, the stitches so small and tight, I had to spread the hairs to locate them. I summoned all the French I had to tell Madame du la Rochelle *merci*.

"C'est bien à votre service, monsieur." She spoke in her smooth contralto while lifting the lid to inspect her biscuits. There was no rancor in her tone. The storm had passed. Living out there, she would be accustomed to resolution.

Steam rose from a chipped enamel basin set up on a chopping block outside the door, where Philippe had hung his capote on the protruding end of a log rafter, rolled up his sleeves, and begun washing his face and hands. I used the outhouse, replenished the water in the basin from a tall kettle standing in a melted hole in the snow, washed up, and while Claude was taking his turn in the outhouse I fed the horses and used my bowie to carve half a pound off the bacon I'd packed on the gray. This gift was met with a bright smile from Fleurette, whose bad teeth subtracted from her good looks, and very soon the smell of frying filled the little dugout. The biscuits were light, absorbing the tasty bacon grease like sponges, and the coffee was thick and strong, the way the French preferred it. I didn't, but it finished waking me up. I asked Philippe about the wound in his back.

"A remembrance of war, *monsieur le depute*. A Canada Firster shot me from the roof of the storehouse in Winnipeg during the Great Rebellion of '69." He crunched bacon.

"Canada Firster?"

"White Protestant whiskey swindlers from Ontario. When they were through getting the Cree drunk and cheating them of the land, they decided to form their own political party. Canada First, nobody second, including Indians, half-breeds, and Roman Catholics." He crossed himself. "We fought them. We lost. *Ce que c'est, que c'est*. What is, is."

"I hear there's another rebellion brewing."

"I have heard the same thing for twelve years. It may brew, but it must brew without Philippe. What fights I fight I fight for my family." He helped himself to a gulp of piping-hot coffee that would have scalded my throat.

I changed the subject. "What kind of country are we heading toward?"

"The worst, *monsieur le depute*. Blizzards,

ice storms, vertical cliffs, hostiles, bandits, wolves, bear, puma, buffalo, moose. It is a mistake not to take the last two seriously. They are savage when surprised or when separated from their young. My wife's brother was crippled by a bull moose in Alberta three years ago." He lowered his voice on the last part, either forgetting or not trusting his statement that Fleurette knew no English. The woman herself, leaning over to wipe Claude's chin with her checked napkin, gave no sign that she understood.

I wiped my own mouth and pushed away my plate. "Let's get started."

The head of the house showed his gold teeth. "You are a man who thirsts for adventure, no?"

"Adventure thirsts for me. If I had my way I'd open a bank and die in my bed at the end of a safe and very dull life. But I'm no hand at arithmetic." I thanked Madame du la Rochelle for another fine meal and rose.

A nomadic Indian might have found fault with the length of time it took the Métis family to gather its gear, secure the homestead, and move out, but any single white man who had observed such an arrangement take place in civilization would have been greatly impressed. From the time Fleurette cleared the plates from the table until we were in the saddle, less than twenty minutes had slid away. This included the following exchange, when Philippe returned from the river leading an enormous dun drafthorse, twenty-two hands at the inside, with a milky eye and white all around its muzzle. It bore a wooden saddle like even no Indian mount had borne since Pizarro shipped home, with three brightly colored blankets beneath it to prevent the clumsy construction from rubbing bloody sores in the beast's hide.

"If you're planning on delivering a shipment of beer to Chipewyan," I said, "you're a little light on barrels."

Philippe grinned from the depths of his hood and stroked the great horse's neck. "King Henry is descended from the mighty steeds of Pepin's stable. He is built to carry eight hundred pounds of armor at full gallop."

"That will come in handy, if the war of the Roses comes back. What about that torture trap of a saddle?"

"I carved it myself from the best white pine. No other will fit his back."

As he spoke, he impressed me by hauling

himself five feet from the ground into the wooden seat and pulled his wife one-handed into the space between him and the packs he had fixed behind the cantle. Fleurette hiked her skirts and rode astride, something no respectable white woman would consider; once aboard she looked as natural and dignified as any banker's wife at a charity social. She wore a gingham bonnet and a coarse woolen cloak that left her arms free to encircle her husband's waist.

"What will Claude ride?" I asked. The boy had on a pilot's cap with a shiny black sealskin visor, lace-up boots, and a capote like his father's that looked as if it had been cut down from an old garment to fit him.

Philippe curled his lip at the question. "I said the boy can run."

"All the way to Fort Chipewyan?"

"Even the horses cannot run that far. You Americans are always in a hurry."

We made thirty miles the first day, a feat I would scarcely have credited when we set out; but high winds had planed the snow flat across the tableland, and whenever I looked back, Claude was always the same distance behind, stepping inside the horses' hoofprints to avoid wallowing in the snow. His face was red — but from cold, not exertion. He was built wiry like his father and had a man's idea of how to pace himself. A single drop of Indian blood is strong enough to turn a bucket of white paint bright scarlet. ✳

The second day we made even better progress. Yesterday's sun had melted some of the snow, and when the temperature plunged at night, it froze a crust strong enough to support even the gray and its packs, creating a pavement as hard and smooth as macadam. The weight of the big dun was too much for it, but the horse's hooves were as large as dinner plates and churned through the broken pieces of crust as if it were meringue. Claude broke into an occasional sprint across the sturdy surface, outdistancing us at times so that his father had to call him back to keep him from blundering into a grizzly or worse. Fleurette rode without complaint, speaking only when addressed by Philippe. Her general silence might have been interpreted as a protest, but I decided that she reserved the energy that might have gone into speaking for the journey. She had gone on record against the expedition, been vetoed, and left it at that. In unity lay survival.

174

Nights we pitched camp, built a fire, and watched Fleurette perform miracles with beans, bacon, and flour in my old skillet while Philippe hauled out a wooden flute no longer than a Sharps cartridge and played tunes going back to the first *coureurs de bois*, trappers and traders who blazed the original Canadian trails a century and more before.

"Runners-in-the-woods," he translated the term between tunes. "Pirates, *monsieur le depute*, trespassing upon territory claimed by the Hudson's Bay Company and the Indians with whom the company traded. Death awaited them from the natives, from whose children's mouths the *coureurs* stole food whenever they pulled in their traps; death awaited them from the company when they blundered into traders. However, one can die but once. They had nothing to lose, and so they went where no white man had gone before. But for them, the whole of Canada would be an empty white smear on the map, populated by dragons and savages with two heads. Ironic, is it not, that I, who am descended from these visionary brigands, should find myself guiding an expedition to bring to justice a band of rogues not unlike them?" He tapped the flute against the sole of one moccasin to clear it of spittle.

"Only if the *coureurs* were in the habit of murdering women and children and burning settlements to the ground for sport," I said.

"A valid point. Those were the tactics of the Hudson's Bay Company."

Claude, seated cross-legged by the fire, looked up briefly from *Wuthering Heights*, then returned to his reading. He had walked and run seventy miles in two days and looked as if he had just finished playing outdoors.

I drank coffee. I was becoming accustomed to the thick strong brew, which seemed to draw the pain from my damaged ribs like whiskey. "When do we reach the next settlement?"

"Three days, if this weather holds." Philippe ran a brown finger along the rim of his delicate moustache. "I would go around it, monsieur."

I remembered what Inspector Vivian had told me in his office in Moose Jaw of the territory beyond the north fork of the Saskatchewan. "Shulamite?"

He nodded. He seemed impressed by my information but too polite to inquire after its source. "It is, perhaps, the first community founded entirely by former slaves since Moses wandered the desert. Needless to say they are not friendly to white Americans."

"This white American fought for the Union."

"Ah, but they know their history. That war was not fought to end slavery, but to establish the authority of Washington City."

"If Bliss and Whitelaw passed near there, would they know it?"

"The wilderness is not a desert, monsieur. It is filled with the noise of life. When strangers pass through it, they create disturbances in the noise, like a stick dragged across the current of a swift stream. That is the natural reality. Beyond that, the woman to whom Shulamite looks for leadership is said to possess second sight. It would not surprise me to learn that she knows of us three already." He studied me from beneath his heavy lids. "It is possible you do not believe in this?"

"The older I get the less I know what I believe. But if this woman has news of Bliss and Whitelaw, I need to talk to her."

"I would be of no assistance in this. Many of their grandfathers were sold to the slave traders by others of their own tribe. The color of one's skin is no guarantee of safe passage."

"If you'll lay out the route, I'll be on my way and send you home. You have a family to protect."

"They will spare us, I think. I would not be a good guide if I did not warn you of the danger to yourself."

"Thank you. I need to talk to the woman."

"In that case, perhaps you would consider giving me that second double eagle now."

I surprised him by producing the leather sack and handing him one of the gold cartwheels. He balanced it upon his palm as if weighing it. Then he gave it to Fleurette, who bit it, studied the result in the firelight, and consigned it to a pocket in the lining of her cloak. Then she returned to her cooking. Philippe lifted his tin cup.

"*Mes compliments,*" he said. "It is a rare wise man who accepts his own mortality."

"One can die but once," I said.

16

Monsieur le depute, I cannot impress upon you too strongly the need for absolute silence."

Philippe's whisper was warm in my ear. I nodded. He lowered his cupped hands then and leaned back into his wooden saddle, wincing when it creaked slightly. He had said nothing to Fleurette riding behind him or Claude standing up to his calves in snow by King Henry's woolly left flank. The boy's labored breath — he had been running — clouded thickly around his head. Both kept silent.

A brush fire had scalped five or six hundred acres of trees sometime within the past year. Crossing that bald country, we had topped a rise overlooking a stream where the forest resumed abruptly. At the base of the hill, standing hock deep in icy water, an enormous shaggy moose raised its head and looked our way, twitching nostrils as big as hen's eggs. Its heavy coat, deep red-brown streaked with black, stretched taut over raw, unfinished muscles that put me in mind of exposed machinery. A ragged beard like a buffalo bull's hung from its chin, shallow beneath the long curved snout and streaming water, and its shovel-shaped antlers spread six feet. The beast would have dressed out at twelve hundred pounds easily — if one could picture its ever placing itself in that position.

Its black eyes, small and almond shaped in nests of wrinkles like an old Indian's, were fixed on the mounted strangers staring at it; but it must have trusted its nose before its eyesight, because after two or three minutes — or hours, take your pick — the great head swung back around and it waded on across the stream slowly and gracefully, mounted the opposite bank with an elegant hop, shook itself with a grunt that reverberated among the trees on that side, and slid in among them without ever looking back. The impression remained that it was aware of us the whole time but didn't estimate us highly enough for hurry.

Thirty more seconds crawled past, then Philippe let out his breath. "A near thing," he said. "The moose, he does not like surprise."

The ground shook suddenly, heavily enough to vibrate up to the seats of our saddles. The great bull crashed out of the brush, pounded down the bank, and smashed into the water, charging straight at us. It raised its head just once, opening its pink mouth with a bawling roar, then lowered its muzzle, nodding as it ran, the huge antlers tipped fully our way like the icebreaker on a snow train. My mustang nickered shrilly and tried to back up, hunching its shoulders to buck when I pulled the reins tight. Out of the corner of my eye I saw the big dun lift its head and look alert for the first time.

Philippe's weapon was a single-shot Springfield carbine he wore slung behind his shoulder. He unlimbered it, but not before I slid the Evans from its scabbard and, squeezing the mustang with my knees, nestled my cheek against the stock and drew a bouncing bead on the broad space between the moose's eyes. The head kept bobbing and I missed the first shot. The Springfield boomed just after; the moose stumbled, found its footing on the near bank, and continued its charge up the slope with a stream of blood glittering between the bunched muscles of its chest.

That was it for the Springfield. The

mustang screamed and twisted away from the onrushing beast. I turned in the saddle, drew a fresh bead, and fired, racking and firing again and again without pausing to see where the slugs were going. I fired a dozen times, the smoke of my own fire obscuring the target, but I squeezed three more into the haze. I heard a grunt like a boulder falling onto soft earth. When the smoke thinned, the moose was on its knees ten feet in front of us, struggling to rise, its antlers tilting right and left with the effort. I took aim again, but by this time Philippe had reloaded. The Springfield boomed, the great head swung around and up with a snap, and dashed to the ground. The shoulders bunched twice as if the will to stand up had outlived the animal itself; then the body sagged on over. One rear leg kicked twice, bent to kick again, and settled into the snow.

The echo of our shots walloped around among the trees for a long time, then growled away like far thunder and died with a hiss.

"*Mon dieu!*" breathed Philippe.

I couldn't think of anything to improve on that.

The moose's musky odor reached us, a swampy stench of heavy sweat and tremendous heat. It did nothing to calm the mustang, and I bailed out, leaning back against the reins when I hit the ground. I fought it for twenty feet until my foot found a burned-over stump under the snow, and I took a hitch around it, knotting it tightly beneath a knob where the grain twisted. Then I retraced my steps to where King Henry stood calm as Sunday with nobody on his back and his reins on the ground. All three du la Rochelles had gathered around the fallen hulk, where Philippe knelt with a butchering knife, carving a chunk out of its coarse-haired rump.

"By Mary, but I wish we were near home," he said. "We would eat for a month."

I said, "You wouldn't have any teeth left at the end of it."

"But you have not tried moose. The meat melts like lard upon your tongue. Afterward the strength of the beast passes into you."

"What made him charge like that? He was safe on his way."

"Who can say? He was an old bull, many times the victor. See those scars upon his shoulders? They are made by the antlers of other bulls who envy his station. One does not survive such a battle unless he who left them perishes. 'This river, and everything you see,' he says perhaps, 'is mine. I shall not share it.' *Un bâtard magnifique,* this fellow. A magnificent bastard." He patted its side. It sounded like someone slapping a drum. "It is a heroic thing to live and die upon one's own terms."

Fleurette said something in which I caught the word *imbecile*. During the quarrel that followed I thought again that she took in far more than she let on.

I noticed Claude then, on his knees in the snow beside the huge carcass, stroking the long stiff hairs that covered its neck. I had yet to hear the boy speak in any language, and wondered if he was mute.

At length, having harvested some steaks and gone inside for the great quivering liver, Philippe packed them securely behind his pine cantle and we crossed the stream, upwind of the moose to mollify the little snake-faced sorrel. The gray, which had stopped below the rise, had neither seen nor smelled anything to upset it, and had held its ground when I let go of the line to wrestle with the mustang. I'd begun to wish I'd traded for another saddle horse when I bought the gray.

After we'd ridden a mile, Philippe asked

me how many times I'd fired at the moose.

"Fifteen."

He thought about that for another twenty or thirty yards. "Hadn't you better reload? There is more than one moose in Canada — and many grizzly."

"I still have eighteen in the magazine."

That kept him silent for a quarter mile.

"This is truly a magical weapon, monsieur," he said then. "What is it called?"

"Evans repeater. They quit making it a couple of years back."

"I should not wonder. A shopkeeper would die of loneliness waiting for a customer to return for more ammunition." He touched his moustache. "I have a cured buffalo robe of unusually fine quality I have been saving. It would bring as much as two hundred dollars in Ottawa. Would you consider trading your Evans repeater for this robe?"

"The gun isn't worth two hundred. When a part wears out you can't replace it."

"I am not without ingenuity in these matters. Will you trade?"

"I may look you up when this is over."

He uncorked his golden grin. "I cannot guarantee this offer will hold, *monsieur le depute*. When this is over there may not be as much need for a rifle that shoots thirty-three times without reloading. The market is, how you say, not stable."

"Thirty-four," I said. "I discharged a round at an escaping prisoner in Montana."

"The robe, monsieur."

"I'd consider it a favor if you stopped calling me monsieur. Deputy Murdock will do, or Murdock if you're in a hurry. The other makes me want to order frog legs in St. Louis."

"I did not intend to commit offense. I await your decision, Deputy Murdock."

"I'll have to see the robe."

"It is in a cedar chest in my cabin."

"In that case I may look you up when this is over."

"You do not trust me, Deputy Murdock?"

I shook my head. "Too many gold teeth."

"Fils de la catin." He spoke beneath his breath.

"I understand a little French," I said.

"I felt certain you did, Deputy Murdock." He put his heels to the big dun and cantered out ahead. Claude sprinted to keep up on foot.

The sun was two hands above the

horizon and still yellow when Philippe drew rein and said we would camp.

"Getting tired?" I asked. "We've got another half hour of daylight."

"That would put us too close, *monsieur le*" — he corrected himself — "Deputy Murdock." He swung down and gave Fleurette his hand to help her out of the saddle.

"Too close to what?"

"Shulamite. Those settlers have lived here for a generation; they can smell strangers an hour away. We do not want to come upon them without sufficient light to defend ourselves."

"The night's as dark for them as it is for us."

"I will not argue. You have hired me to guide you. If you will not accept this guidance, I will return to you your double eagles and leave you to your fate. Perhaps the wolves will have left me a portion of that moose."

"You ought to write ten-cent dreadfuls, Philippe. Your talent's wasted in this rough country." But I stepped out of leather and went back to unpack the gray.

We built a small fire to avoid attracting undue notice, and Fleurette cooked the moose, which was as good as Philippe had said. After supper, he produced his wooden flute and stretched one leg to jostle his son, who was dozing over his book, with the toe of his moccasin. " 'Ma Petit Marie,' Claude, eh?"

Instantly the boy was awake, his sunburned face bright with anticipation. He listened to his father tootling the opening bars of some bright tune I had never heard, lips moving slightly as if he were counting the beats, then opened his mouth and sang, in a pure, clean soprano:

> *Au printemps,*
> *l'été, l'automne,*
> *et passer par tous l'hiver,*
> *je promene la ruelle*
> *avec ma petit Marie.*

When the song was finished, Philippe barked a short laugh of Gallic pride, leaned forward, and, taking Claude by his ears, pulled him close and kissed him on both cheeks. When he let go with a push, the boy nearly fell over on his back. His father turned his bright dark eyes on me.

"A *protégé*, is he not? If we but lived in Paris, he would be the toast of a continent."

"*Et pas Métis*," put in his wife.

"Oui." Philippe nodded, the brightness fading. "And were we not Métis."

"I'd made up my mind the boy couldn't speak," I said.

"There is no need for speech when one can sing like the angels."

"Angels you all be, iffen you don't keep still."

This was a new voice, harsh and deep, and belonged to a scarecrow figure that had materialized against a night sky made pale by starshine reflected from the snow. The figure itself was dead black, as if it were gathered from the darkness the sky had surrendered. For punctuation, an angular elbow straightened and bent with a jerk, accompanied by the crisp metallic crackle of a shell jacking into the chamber of a lever-action carbine.

17

We remained quiet. Not even Fleurette made so much as a gasp. We kept our places around the fire and watched as another figure, this one shorter and broader, joined the first, and then a third came into the group, all armed with rifles and carbines. At length an arc of orange light crept above the bulge where they stood, and rose like a miniature dawn swinging from a bail in the hand of a fourth party who appeared to carry no weapons. The lantern painted glistening stripes along the long guns' oiled barrels and made ovals of the facial features beneath the floppy brims of the newcomers' hats. I was not much surprised to find they were black faces, male and grim as open graves.

"This the bunch, Brother Enoch?" asked the man with the lantern. His voice was a gentle rumble, oddly soothing.

Enoch, evidently the scarecrow who had appeared first, stirred himself. But the question was answered by a fifth man who slid out of the shadows on the other side of our camp; a man nearly as large as all the others put together, who made no noise at all when he walked. He carried a full-length Sharps big-bore rifle that looked like a boy's squirrel gun in his huge hands.

"There's only three horses," he said. His voice was light for his size.

The man with the lantern nodded. "I'll have your weapons. Take them out slowly and throw them into the light."

I unholstered the Deane-Adams between thumb and forefinger and flipped it onto the ground near his feet. Philippe slid the Springfield carbine from beneath his blankets and tossed it after. I had my Winchester leaning against my saddle, which I was using for a backrest, and the Evans lying alongside. I added them to the pile.

"The woman and the boy are unarmed, monsieur," Philippe said.

The lantern came up a little, spreading its light over Philippe's face. "You Métis?" The rumbling tones smoothed out another notch.

"*Oui*. Yes. The woman is my wife and the boy is my son."

Now the lantern swept slowly across the others and stopped. I squinted against the glare.

"Who's this, your brother?" Now there was nothing soothing about the man's speech.

I'd been working on a number of answers to just that question since the moment I'd made my decision to stop at Shulamite, but I discarded them all in favor of the truth, which required less effort to maintain. "The name is Murdock," I said. "I'm a deputy United States marshal in pursuit of a gang of fugitives wanted in Montana Territory."

Enoch took in his breath with a little rattle, like a snake's. I got the impression then he was consumptive. That would explain his thinness. In the lantern light the skin of his face barely covered the bone. "I knowed he was some kind of law. They all gots that mean look."

"Any of these fugitives happen to be black?" asked the man with the lantern.

"Not that I know of. One of the leaders is half Mexican. The other's Cherokee."

"That sounds mighty like a description of Lorenzo Bliss and Charlie Whitelaw."

"You've seen them?" I asked.

The man with the lantern shook his head. "Read about them. Brother Enoch goes to Fort Chipewyan once a month for needs and possibles. He brings back the

Ottawa newspapers when the Mounties are through with them. Does it surprise you to learn a black man can read?" There was no hostility in his tone. The words carried all that was necessary.

"Some of the places I've lived I was surprised to meet a white man who could. We all have the same opportunities."

He laughed then, loudly, deeply, and entirely without amusement. Then he stopped. His face more than the others' was a mass of ovals, turned this way and that to represent nose, cheeks, forehead, and chin, as if it were assembled from identical machine parts, with each part moving independently of the rest. When he spoke and laughed, only his mouth moved. When he registered curiosity or surprise, his forehead shifted upward like a typewriter carriage. "It's a good thing you didn't lie about where you came from, Marshal. Only a white American could say what you just said without spitting."

"I didn't mean to offend."

That brought about the shift of the forehead mentioned above. He could tell I hadn't said it just because he held my life in his hands. "My name is Hebron," he said. "I am the elected leader of the free African community of Shulamite, of which these four gentlemen comprise the Committee of Public Vigilance. I am telling you this so you don't take the idea you've been unlawfully abducted. You are all under arrest and will come with us."

"What's the charge?" I asked.

His mouth formed a smile, again without amusement. "In your case, trespassing while white. These others are your aides and abetters."

"Will there be a trial?"

"Possess your soul in patience, Marshal. All things will be known in the fullness of God's time."

I'd attended church often enough to take that to mean he didn't know the answer to the question.

The men formed a circle around us with their rifles and carbines at hip level while we saddled up and I untied the packs from the tree where I'd hoisted them out of the reach of bears and wolves and secured them on the gray. Hebron insisted that Claude ride behind me on the mustang so they could keep an eye on him. Ropes were produced and Philippe's hands and mine were tied to our saddle horns. The big man, whose name was Brother Babel, brought the men's horses — older mounts mostly, some as old as King Henry, but

well fed and groomed to a high shine —
and without awaiting instructions the
riders split into escort formation, three in
back and two in front, the leaders taking
charge of our reins while one of the men at
the rear led the gray. Four of them rode
bareback, but I noticed that Hebron strad-
dled a McClellan. That, and the way he
rode, back straight and elbows in — suggested cavalry experience. That explained
the formation, which came right out of the
section on prisoners in the manual of
arms; I'd used pages torn from it to light
fires during the winter of 1863.

I don't know why — never having seen
one outside of a framed lithograph hanging
on a wall in Judge Blackthorne's private
study — but whenever I'd thought about
Shulamite I'd pictured a walled city, with
or without a moat to repel invaders. But
there was nothing medieval or even forbid-
ding about the scatter of log buildings that
greeted us as we followed the long gentle
slope to the S-shaped river at its base, the
buildings black against the snow, with
lighted windows hanging among them like
pinecones. It might have been any settlement of trappers or miners, carved from
the evergreen forests that surrounded it,
with a large meeting hall standing more or

less in its center and a watchtower affair built like a derrick with a roofed platform for spotting Indians and fires.

Hebron drew rein fifty yards short of the riverbank, raising one hand for the others to do the same. Enoch, seated to his right, lifted his carbine from across his lap — I saw now it was a Spencer — pointed it skyward, and fired. The echo of the report was still snarling in the distance when a puff of smoke answered from the high platform, followed closely by the crack of a rifle. Hebron's hand came down then and we crossed the river. The water was just fetlock high, but there were ice shards glittering in the current and I had to kick the sorrel twice before it would step off the bank. I knew by the sound of its snort as it made contact with the water that I would pay later. King Henry, the big dun of chivalric stock, crossed without protest.

The buildings were laid out in two ragged rows alongside a rude street, bare of snow and ringing like iron beneath the shoes of the horses. I saw heads silhouetted in the windows, but no one came out, as might normally be expected in a remote settlement when strangers entered. The man in the tower, outlined against the square of sky between the roof and the platform, turned as we rode past, the barrel of his rifle following us like the head of a coiled snake. I felt uncommonly white. I had experienced that same sensation years before, when I had entered a hostile Cheyenne village as the captive of the chief; but even on that occasion, the warriors and their women had stepped outside their lodges to stare at me, and packs of nondescript yellow dogs had come trotting alongside to yip and snap at my heels. Of all the places I had visited, of my own free will and otherwise, Shulamite alone met me with only silence. I thought that if someone would take a shot at me I'd welcome the variety.

At length we stopped before the big meeting hall, if that's what it was, and Hebron handed Enoch King Henry's lead and stepped down and tied his slat-sided chestnut to the hitching rail in front. A shallow flight of steps made from half-sawn logs led to a porch that ran the length of the building, but unlike similar porches on ranch houses across the American West this one contained no rockers or gliders or anything else to indicate that the porch was used for anything other than to keep rain and snow off whoever crossed to the door. Hebron knocked at the door, waited, then went inside.

My fingers were numb, either from the cold or from the tightness of the ropes binding my wrists. I asked Enoch if I could step down while we were waiting. He didn't answer or even turn his head to show he'd heard. He coughed a little — the phlegmy, hollow-lunged cough of the consumptive — but it wasn't intended as a response. He hadn't spoken since Hebron had made his appearance.

In a little while the door opened again and Hebron stepped out. In the light coming from the window on either side he was a middle-built man of about my age, with a black goatee trimmed close to his chin, a broad mouth, and sad eyes — or eyes anyway that didn't appear to expect much beyond more of what they'd already seen. He wore, in addition to the floppy farmer's hat that seemed to be a uniform among his group, a sheepskin coat with the fleece turned in, heavy woolen trousers stuffed into the tops of high lace-up boots like lumbermen wore, a flannel shirt, and a broad belt with a U.S. Army buckle, which backed up my supposition about his cavalry training. All of these items had seen their share of wear — scuffed, faded, torn, and patched — but they were clean and well kept, the belt and boots shining with oil and the brass buckle polished. Whatever the nature of his service was, it had taken.

He had been wearing leather gauntlets, which he had taken off inside. He seemed to realize he was still holding them and stuffed them into his belt. Then he pointed at me. "The others can wait. She wants to see you."

"Who does?" I asked.

He showed surprise for the first time, edged with contempt for my ignorance.

"Queen Fidelity," he said. "Who else would *she* be?"

18

Enoch dismounted and used a narrow-bladed knife of Indian manufacture to slice through the ropes on my wrists. I worked my fingers and when the pins and needles went away gripped the horn and swung down to the ground. Hebron, who still showed no weapons, stepped aside from the door, motioning me to enter ahead of him. I climbed the steps and obeyed.

The interior of the lodge — it was too big to call a cabin — was darker than outdoors, lit only by scattered candles and a hurricane lamp suspended from the rafters by a rope smeared with glistening tar. As my eyes adjusted I made out the oblong shapes of long trestle tables arranged in rows on either side of the door with a wide aisle leading between them to the back. The room was apparently a combination meeting place and dining hall; the odor of roasted meat and old grease was too strong to have come from just the tallow candles.

At the end of the aisle, the head of a

moose at least as large as the one Philippe and I had shot, but whose antlers spanned a good eight feet, decorated the wall above a door cut from the boards that surrounded it. The reflected glow of the room's tiny flames in the glass eyes, and the crawling play of shadows, made the head seem as if it were still alive. Knowing that it wasn't didn't do a thing to prevent my stomach from tying itself into a clammy knot.

I followed Hebron to the end of the aisle, where he tapped softly on the door. There was a muffled response from the other side. He took off his hat, exposing a receding hairline of tight curls with silver glittering in them, and jerked his chin. I understood and removed my badger headpiece. The great room was unheated; dank cold touched my scalp. He pulled open the door and once again stood aside for me to go through first. I did so, and was blinded by the light.

I had been to St. Louis, where the finer homes, hotels, and saloons were lit by gas, bright as day where the proprietors were not overly concerned with the cost. None of these establishments was brighter than this room. Candles of every shape and size — some tall, thin, and aristocratic, others short and squat as toads, still others carved into human silhouettes — burned on trays and in jars on pedestals and shelves and along a narrow raised platform against the far wall, dripping wax onto the black cloth that covered the last, filling the place with light and the smell of hot wax; no tallow here. The smoke rose and roiled around among the rafters, which like those in the great hall were fifteen feet above the floor, with no ceiling to contain the heat. Even so the room was warm enough from just the candles to make me unbutton the bearskin I was wearing. The walls were undecorated, bare logs with a window on either side covered by more black cloth. The room was less than half the size of the other, which made it plenty spacious, but the atmosphere was as oppressive as if I were standing in an airtight closet. It made my skin crawl and made me drowsy at the same time. It was well past midnight, but the effect would be the same at high noon. In here the sun would rise and fall without notice or importance.

The least impressive thing about the room was the old woman who sat in a spindle-backed rocker in front of the platform, a shrunken Negress with a cap of white hair wrapped in a worn and ragged shawl, a thick steamer rug draped over her knees and hanging down to cover her feet. Her face was as brown and wrinkled as a shriveled apple and showed no life beyond a pair of rimless spectacles whose thick lenses seemed to gather the light from the candles. When she moved her head slightly, the flash raked my eyes as if someone had swept a bull's-eye lantern across them. Apart from that she might have been carved from the same wax as the candles, and beginning to melt from the heat.

A stretch of silence went by, during which I heard a thousand wicks burning. When she opened her mouth to speak, I saw the pink of her gums. She had no teeth.

"What is your name?"

"Murdock."

She shook her head, semaphores flashing off her spectacles. "What is your *Christian* name?"

She pronounced the *h* in *Christian* and flicked her tongue off the floor of her mouth on the *r*. She had not learned English in America or Canada.

"Page."

She repeated the name silently, her lips touching on the *P*. Her hands moved then, sliding a small book bound in tattered black cloth from beneath the rug that covered her lap. It might have been a pocket Bible. Tissue-thin pages slithered between fingers as wrinkled as ill-fitting gloves. She moved her lips as she read. Finally she looked up, adjusting her glasses.

"A name of French derivation. I assume you know what it means."

It wasn't a Bible. "My father told me my grandfather was through using it."

"It means 'attendant on a noble.' Which noble do you attend?"

"That would be Judge Blackthorne." When she went on staring at me without response I said, "Harlan Blackthorne."

Pages slithered.

"Prussian. 'From the land of warriors.' This is appropriate?"

"Oh, yes, ma'am."

"My name is Queen Fidelity. You will address me by my full name at all times."

"What does it mean?"

" 'Faithfulness.' I assure you it is appropriate." She put the book — and her hands — back under cover. "Brother Hebron, see that the three people who accompanied Page Murdock are made comfortable."

Hebron said, "I'll tell Brother Enoch."

"See to it yourself. I wish to have a private audience with Page Murdock."

"That's not a good idea."

A cross of white light leapt off the spectacles. "Your opinion of my ideas is of no interest to me. Move them into Chapter Six."

"That's my cabin!"

"I said I wish them to be comfortable."

The silence that followed was twice as long as the first. No two buffalo bulls ever butted heads with more determination. Hebron blinked first. The door closed softly behind him.

"The people of Shulamite are former slaves and the sons and daughters of slaves," she said when we were alone. "It is a small community now. Most of the original settlers returned to America after emancipation. Those who voted to remain did so because they would not reconcile with a nation that would allow this monstrous evil to exist for two hundred and forty years. They are at war with the United States."

"They're short on manpower if they mean to make any kind of fight."

"It is a defensive war. They do not invade. They slay invaders."

"I fought for the Union."

"You fought for the Union. You did not

fight to end slavery."

"It's the same thing."

She touched her spectacles. I was a difficult student. "All the other civilized nations volunteered to abandon the practice of taking and keeping slaves without having to shed blood over the issue. It took a war to show you the evil, and even then you fought only because you were attacked."

"You don't know that about me."

"Nor do they." She spread her hands, showing the pale palms. "For four years the enemy wore gray. Now they must go by skin alone."

"You consider that fair?"

"They did not set the precedent. You did."

It was like arguing with that warrior Judge Blackthorne.

"What about my friends?"

"Your friends are Métis. The free African community of Shulamite is not at war with the native peoples of the Dominion of Canada. They will be free to go in the morning. Tonight they are guests."

"And me?"

"Your fate is in the hands of Brother Hebron and the Committee of Public Vigilance. I never interfere with them unless I am invited."

"Aren't you their leader?"

"Brother Hebron is their leader, with the assistance of the committee. I advise the residents of Shulamite upon spiritual matters only. I am *mambo* here."

"Mambo?"

"Priest, healer, exorcist, sayer of the sooth. I also organize public entertainments and train the choir. We have a soprano who shows promise for the spring planting services if his testicles do not drop before then."

She sounded exactly like the Reverend Royden Milsap of the First Presbyterian Church in Helena.

"You're a preacher," I said.

"I am *mambo*."

"Christian?"

She shook her head. *"Voudoun."*

My ignorance must have showed on my face, because she opened her mouth in a toothless pink grin I can still see when I close my eyes.

"Voodoo," she said.

19

Brother Hebron will take you to your quarters."

It was a dismissal — and a disappointment. In view of her late announcement of her religious denomination, her own disappearance in a puff of green smoke would have been more appropriate.

I left Queen Fidelity alone with her book of names and found Hebron waiting for me in the gloom of the great hall. His mood went with the atmosphere. He didn't take to having been turned out like some kind of servant, particularly with me as a witness. He made no remark as he escorted me back down the front steps and, accompanied by the members of the Committee of Public Vigilance, across a stretch of snow-covered field as flat as a parade ground to a tiny building constructed of the same pine logs as all the rest, with a slant roof and no windows. The moon had risen and the entire settlement was lit as brightly as at noon.

The door was secured with a plain block of wood that turned on a nail. Enoch turned it straight up and down and the door fell open on leather hinges. Hebron relieved one of the others of the lantern he had been carrying earlier and waited for me to go in first.

The inside smelled dankly of decaying wood. When Hebron entered with the lantern I saw that it was a storage building for rakes and hoes and a wicked-looking scythe like the one Death carried in fanciful illustrations in the copies of the *New York Herald* that arrived at Judge Blackthorne's chambers once a month in bales. Bushel baskets nested inside one another in one corner, and jars of nails and square bottles of horse liniment lined a shelf built across the back wall. Even without the clutter there would have been barely enough room for Hebron and me both to stand inside. Brother Babel would have poked out a log with an elbow the first time he had an itch to scratch.

"Lean back against that wall and fold your arms across your chest."

I did as directed, using the only wall that wasn't supporting some piece of long-handled equipment. He hung the lantern on a nail, gathered a double armload of tools, and thrust them through the door at Enoch, who turned his head toward Babel, the biggest man in the group — in *any* group — who stepped forward to take them.

That exchange told me most of what I needed to know about Brother Enoch. A second-in-command who passed the menial work on to others wasn't planning to remain second-in-command forever. I wondered if having figured that out was going to do me any good.

Hebron looked at the bushel baskets and the jars and liniment, decided apparently that they were harmless in my possession, and gave me the presidential stare.

"You'll sleep here tonight. I wouldn't advise anything bold and reckless, like trying to kick your way through the door. You and the door will both be shot full of holes at the first blow. I won't lose any sleep over you, but making and hanging a new door takes time and it's already a twenty-four-hour-a-day job bringing a settlement this size through the winter." He stuck a foot outdoors.

"Can I trouble you for my bedroll?" The floor was bare earth and frozen hard as stone.

He considered the question. He was a

thinking leader. I'd heard that was what had cost Jefferson Davis the Confederacy.

"I'll see what I can do. This ain't the Palmer House."

That was the first chink that had opened in his carefully constructed English. He saw that I noticed and if a black man can flush I swear that's what happened. "Mind what I said about those guards."

Once again I caught him on the fly. "What will they do to me that won't be done tomorrow anyway?"

"You don't know that. Neither do we. We'll decide tonight. In any case I never knew a man who wouldn't put it off until later if he could."

He left, taking the lantern with him. The door thumped shut and the block of wood squeaked into place. I was alone in the darkest place I had ever been.

I stood my fur collar up against the dank cold and explored my options.

I groped for one of the square bottles and pulled the cork with my teeth. The sharp fumes stung my nostrils and made my eyes water. I dug out the little oilcloth bundle I kept in a pocket, removed a match, struck it against the rough bark on a log, and touched it to the bottle's thick rim. A blue flame flickered.

I blew it out, stuck the cork back in, and returned the liniment to the shelf. If I splashed the contents over the wall at the back of the building and set the logs afire, the flames just might have burned through before dawn, by which time I'd have choked to death from the smoke. Even if I survived and got past the guards, I'd have to make my way to a horse, and since I had no firearms or provisions, the Canadian wilderness would only finish what the flames and the guard would have started. I pocketed the matches and sat down on the skirts of my coat with my back against the wall and my knees drawn up to my chest for warmth. The building wasn't big enough for me to stretch out even if I'd wanted to.

When the door came open it startled me from a doze. I didn't know how long I'd been out. Hebron was back with the lantern and my bedroll.

"Don't get up." He hung up the one, tossed the other on the ground, and upended one of the stout bushel baskets to serve as a stool. When he sat down and pushed his hat back with a knuckle, he appeared more relaxed than he had since we'd met. He looked at me with the machinery of his thoughts working behind his face. Then he unbuttoned a pocket on his flannel shirt and drew out a leadfoil pack of ready-made cigarettes and a box of matches.

He held out the pack. I shook my head. "I never got the habit."

He speared one between his lips and set fire to it. He counted the cigarettes remaining in the pack before he put it away.

"I've had good reasons to wish I'd done the same," he said. "No matter how careful I am about it I always run out a week or so before one of us makes the monthly trip to Fort Chipewyan for supplies. Some winters the month between runs ninety days. Then there's the cost."

"I never heard anyone who uses tobacco complain about the price."

"That's three cents a pack that could be spent on candy for the children. Life up here is hard for the small ones. It's like burning up the one thing they might have to look forward to."

"Cheaper to buy the makings and roll your own."

He let the cigarette droop and held out his hands. The palms were shiny with callus and the knuckles were swollen as big as walnuts. I understood then why he didn't carry a gun; he'd have had to file off the guard to get one of those fingers close to the trigger.

"Rolling your own requires dexterity. I took rheumatism cutting cane in Mississippi for fifteen years. Some days I can't bend my hands around a pick handle."

I didn't say anything to that. The lantern was putting out heat, but the air inside the building felt as cold as it had at the start. He was being too friendly. Anyone can manage to work up affection for the soon-to-be extinct. Sometime while I was asleep a decision had been reached.

"How long have you been behind a badge?" he asked me then.

"Coming on six years."

"I guess a man has to be able to take care of himself to hang on so long in that line. Deputies especially; they get all the muddy work. I know a little about that. I was a sergeant with the Tenth Cavalry."

"I figured something on that order. I rode cavalry during the war."

"I was infantry then. Thirty-sixth Colored. I was among the first to sign on with the Tenth when they were putting it together."

"That was after the war. Then you didn't come up here as a slave."

He flicked a scrap of glowing ash at the ground, then returned the cigarette to its groove in his lower lip. "No, I didn't."

Seeing the barricade across that road, I asked him if the Committee of Public Vigilance had settled my case.

"We're going to put you in with Brother Babel. You know which one Babel is?"

I nodded. "Pike's Peak with a hat."

"The last time he changed hands as a slave, he sold for a thousand dollars. That's five times what a prime specimen of healthy buck brought on the Virginia market. It was a bargain. The first time he tried to ride a mule it bucked him. He got up, shook the dust off his pants, picked up the mule, and threw it. That's not a story. I saw him do it."

"I'm supposed to fight him with what?"

"Your hands." He spat out smoke. "It was Brother Enoch's idea."

"I was pretty sure I wasn't popular with him."

"Nothing personal. There was nothing personal about taking slaves either."

"Where'd he get this idea?"

"He was just a boy when Sherman burned the plantation where he worked with his mother. His father went down the river to auction before Enoch was old

215

enough to remember what he looked like. Whenever two bucks got into a fight, the overseer broke it up and told them to work out their differences in the barn. He invited his friends and took bets, just like at a cockfight. Usually one of the brawlers took a beating and gave up. Occasionally one died. When that happened, the overseer had to pay the owner of the plantation for the loss of a good field hand, but he usually made enough laying bets to make a profit even then."

"Then the free African community of Shulamite is just a plantation with the colors reversed."

"What did you expect, some kind of noble experiment? Everything we learned about governing we learned from the white man."

I said nothing. He smoked the cigarette short enough to singe his fingers, then dropped it and pressed it out with the toe of his boot. "I didn't vote in favor of it, if that means anything. I wanted to shoot you and be done with it. I've got no stomach for drawing things out."

"What did Queen Fidelity say?"

"She never takes a hand in these things unless she's invited."

"How did you wind up with a voodoo

witch for a priest?"

"All the Negro ministers we knew preached the white man's gospel. Voodoo belongs to us. I can't say I care much for it. The ceremonies give me a headache and are a waste of good chickens besides. When I cut one up, it's to eat. But then I wasn't much of a Christian, either. Turning the other cheek is what got us over here to begin with."

"Whose decision was it to name you all after cities in the Bible?"

"Not all. Some of us hung on to the names we used in the States. The women especially. Those who decided to change chose the Old Testament. It got Jesus out of the picture and the names were easier to pronounce than African. Queen Fidelity's the only one here who ever even saw that place. She left Capetown, where the competition was too thick to make a living, and got run out of Philadelphia and Baltimore by witch burners. She came up here from the American territories ten or twelve years ago. You need women to make religion take and there weren't enough of them down there." He dug out the cigarette pack, but just to play with; the cigarettes stayed inside. "She spends most of her time casting spells to help the crops."

"Do any good?"

"Most of the Shulamites seem to be of that opinion. I suspect we'd have the same number of droughts and blights and bumpers with or without her dead chickens, and have that many more eggs to eat without. A lot of our people came straight up here on the Underground without learning anything of the world on the way, so it makes as much sense to them as the miracle at Cana. My thought is anyone who could make wine out of water ought to have figured out a way to come down off that cross."

"I've been wondering where you took your schooling."

He showed his teeth in an idiot's grin.

"Ain't all us nigras as dumb as rocks, boss. I had me the benefit of a master who taught the classics at Jefferson before he retired to the genteel ways of the gentleman farmer. I reckon I was his pet. He showed me how to read the Bible in English and then Caesar in Latin. It got me out of the canebrakes, so I didn't put up no holler. I dipped me a toe in Homer, too, but he was all Greek to me. Hee-hee."

His imitation of a whiny coon set my teeth on edge. "You don't have to do that. I'd have asked the same of any white man this side of Chicago who talked like Mat-thew Arnold. Most of them can't manage *Frank Leslie's Illustrated Newspaper*."

"I beg your pardon. We aren't equal no matter what John Brown said. When someone says something *you* don't take to, you've got the privilege of thinking he just doesn't like you. I've got to figure in being black as well."

"I wish I could say for sure your being black didn't have anything to do with what I said."

"You're honest, and that's a fact." He took out a cigarette this time and lit it. "Who'd you ride with in the war?"

"Rosecrans."

"Army of the Cumberland. I heard he was good. Lincoln almost put him in charge of the whole shebang."

"It would've been a mistake. He was a stubborn Kraut, and he read too much his-tory. He'd have thrown away the best we had defending Little Roundtop with a copy of Napoleon's *Maxims* in one hand."

He smoked for a moment in silence. "I fought the Cheyenne in Nebraska."

"I fought them in Dakota. They were worth fighting."

"I deserted."

I let that one drop all the way to the

ground. "I guess you had your reasons."

"I thought so at the time. After Custer and the Seventh wiped out Black Kettle at the Washita I couldn't see celebrating my freedom by making slaves of some people I didn't have any complaint with. That's how I wound up here. I'll warrant there's a firing squad waiting for me at Fort Kearney."

"In that case you were right to keep running once you started. The army used up all its sharpshooters in the war. What's left would shoot you in all the places that didn't count and some lieutenant would have to walk up and put a ball in your head with his side arm."

"I wouldn't mind too much if the lieutenant was Henry Flipper. He's a Negro, first one to graduate West Point. I never knew him, though; he came after I left. I read about it in the *Toronto Mail*. Could be he's whiter than some whites. They tell me that can happen when you live among them." He got rid of some ash. "But even if it was him and he was black through and through, I wouldn't take to being shot for a coward. The cowardly thing would have been to stick and keep on doing what I'd been. Most of the brave things that are done get done because someone was more afraid not to do them."

"That may be your problem," I said. "Too much education."

"There isn't a day goes by I don't cuss out that damn schoolteacher."

The lantern began to flicker. It was running low. He stood up, turned down the wick, and took the lantern off its nail. He looked down at me from the doorway.

"Not that it will do you any good," he said. "There's a stronghold on Cree Lake up north where some of Sitting Bull's Sioux live. They didn't turn themselves in with the old man and they're pledged to fight to the death to avoid going back to America. We trade with them sometimes. Brother Zoan speaks a little Sioux and is friendly with their leader, Wolf Shirt. He's been known to offer hospitality to desperadoes from below the border."

All the cold went out of me then. "Did your Brother Zoan see Lorenzo Bliss and Charlie Whitelaw there?"

"He hasn't been there in a month, but when a door opens for a man on the run, it doesn't take him long to find it. I'd look for your fugitives there before I went anywhere else."

"Wolf Shirt would have to be worse than Geronimo to harbor a bunch like that."

221

"Whitelaw being Cherokee would help. It's a Sioux trait to look down on every tribe that isn't Sioux, but they don't hate the others the way they hate Americans. Americans at war with America are another story. That's why Wolf Shirt trades with us. The fact that Bliss and Whitelaw are wanted would only sweeten the pot. Indians will do just about anything to inconvenience the big chief in Washington."

"Do the Mounties know this?"

"If they don't, they will. Canada has no beef against the Sioux for what happened to Custer, but after what this gang did on the Saskatchewan, the Mounties would track them through hell and fight the devil on his own ground."

"That's the first good thing I've heard you say about a bunch of white men."

"*Canadian* white men. Canada never took slaves."

"Thank you for the information. I'll follow up on it just as soon as I finish with Brother Babel."

He looked down at me from the doorway, sucking on his cigarette.

"Babel has long arms," he said then. "As long as your legs. Some men try to stay outside their reach. That's a mistake when you don't have room to run. You want to get inside them if you plan to do any damage."

"You betting on me?"

He dropped the butt and squashed it out, shaking his head. "If anyone in Shulamite had money to bet with I wouldn't put mine on you, and there aren't any takers on Babel. He'll kill you, all right. I'd just like to see someone in your situation get a better chance than those chickens."

20

I actually slept the rest of the night. I'm an old man now, and wakefulness has never been among my maladies. It might have been then, if I'd had any hope of surviving a fight with Brother Babel. When you know how a thing is going to come out and that nothing you do will change it, you can stop thinking and rest. I wrapped myself in my blanket, tugged the badger hat down over my ears, put my head down on my knees — and the next thing I knew there was sunlight sifting through the places where the chinking had fallen out from between the logs and the noises outside of a settlement coming to life.

The door opened and Brother Enoch stood just outside it with his Spencer across his thighs while a man whose name I didn't know, but who had been present among the members of the Committee of Public Vigilance when our camp was broken, set a tin cup of steaming coffee and a plate heaped with scrambled eggs on the ground inside my reach. That meant at least one of Queen Fidelity's chickens hadn't yet gone to the altar.

Smelling the eggs, I realized I was famished. I shoveled them in using the wooden cooking spoon provided and drove the chill out of my bones with the hot coffee, either one of which would have passed muster in San Francisco; as indefensible as slavery was, it had taught some talented people a good trade.

"Let's don't keep Brother Babel waiting," said Enoch when I set aside the plate and cup. "He ain't as patient as he looks."

He and the other man flanked me to the meeting hall. The sky, clear yesterday, had turned the color of tarnished silver and rolled down almost to the ground. A dull pain in my cracked ribs, nearly healed now, told me we were in for a change in the weather. The air smelled and tasted of iron.

They had shoved and stacked the trestle tables against the walls in the great dining room and uncovered the windows, but the gray sunlight was inadequate, and so pitch-smeared torches burned in brackets and a wagon-wheel fixture with lanterns attached hung from the center rafter, casting pools of shadow at the feet of the assembled citizens of Shulamite. There were right around a hundred of them, the men in overalls and flannel, the women in print dresses and gingham, all homespun. The collected years of enforced servitude had taught them all the skills necessary for a community to survive amid the desolation of unsettled territory. No cry went up when I entered with my escort, and no cheer either when Babel came in a few minutes later, attended by another member of the committee; the spectators remained silent in their wide circle, their faces as solemn as the jury they were. This was no sporting event but an execution.

I looked for Philippe, Fleurette, and Claude, wondering if they had left as Queen Fidelity had promised. I spotted them finally near the south wall, the woman and the boy standing atop one of the tables to see above the heads of the crowd. Philippe nodded slightly when our eyes met. His expression was grave.

No one stood along the west wall. There below the stuffed moose head hung a black cloth the size of a bedsheet, with a chalk drawing on it of a cross with a skull and crossbones suspended beneath the axis, surrounded by symbols that meant nothing to me. It might have been painted by a moderately talented child. In front of the cloth sat Queen Fidelity in her rocker. The effect of those stacked heads — moose, skull, old hag — was comical and ghastly at the same time. She looked exactly as she had the night before, in spectacles, ratty shawl, and steamer rug. A fixture of the building, she might have been picked up, chair and all, in the adjoining room and set down on that spot without stirring.

She could have been mistaken for an ebony carving for all the life she showed as I was led to the center of the plank floor and stopped with a prod of Enoch's Spencer. Babel joined me a moment later, and we stood four feet apart without speaking. He had on loose woolen trousers held up by braces and a faded striped shirt made from enough material for two garments of ordinary size. His bare feet were as big as skillets and gripped the floor as if they had been bolted in place. My head came to his breastbone. I could have hidden behind his bulk on the back of the little mustang. His big face was blank; given the atmosphere of black magic, I might have thought he was in some kind of trance if I hadn't attended my share of prizefights and seen that same lack of expression on the faces of the combatants. There were no thoughts in that great inverted kettle of a head beyond those connected with my annihilation.

Most of the details of the ceremony that preceded the fight were lost to me, busy as I was attempting to attain that same mental state in regard to Babel. When Queen Fidelity arose finally, with the assistance of a woman on each side wrapped in an identical white sheet secured at the shoulders with pins, she was barely taller than she had been sitting. Behind the chair, nearly touching the cloth, stood the black-covered platform I had seen in the other room, moved there and set up with a collection of clay vessels arranged at precise intervals in a straight line. She lifted the largest of the jugs and, raising it above her head, offered it to the four directions, the way I had seen Indian shamans do with a medicine pipe. As she did so she recited something in a singsong language that I identified belatedly as English, sprinkled with foreign terms such as *loa, rada,* and *petro.* Lowering the jug, she turned and poured some of its contents into each of three smaller jars on the platform, muttering something that I thought at the time sounded like Father, Son, and Holy Ghost, though I don't credit it now. After setting down the big jug she took a handful of sand or coarsely ground flour from another vessel, then turned and stepped in front of her chair and let it sift out the bottom of her fist to the floor in a rotating motion, so that the pattern roughly resembled the shape of the skull painted on the black cloth behind the platform. Then she stood aside while the two women in sheets came forward — or rather backward, as they advanced with their backs turned away from the wall — until they stood on either side of the crude skull on the floor.

The planks beneath my feet began to vibrate. The spectators stamped their feet in a precise three-beat rhythm — blam blam *blam,* blam blam *blam* — like fists beating a drum, only amplified by the number of beaters and with the inescapably eerie effect of a hundred people acting in unison without a signal and without one foot missing the beat. It made my scalp move.

While this was going on, the women in white gyrated to the rhythm, twisting their torsos and snaking their arms about their head, but without moving their feet, which were bare and like Babel's fixed to the floor. The dance itself looked joyful, but whenever I glimpsed their faces, they were glued into the motionless empty grin of the skull on the cloth and the skull on the floor. The room began to fill with the heat of overactive bodies and the thick musk of sweat. I began to feel woozy, and wondered if the breakfast I'd eaten had contained some kind of drug. I was pretty sure it didn't, and that the ceremony was not meant to upset me before the fight. It all had the feeling of something that had been done many times before, that no longer needed rehearsal. For all I knew, they did it before every event, even the ordinary ones, like Christians saying grace before eating.

Some, I noticed, did not take part in the stamping. These included Brother Hebron and the members of the Committee of Public Vigilance, who stood in one corner with their arms folded and their eyes on Brother Babel and me. I couldn't tell whether they disapproved of the ceremony or were indifferent to it, or if they were just waiting for the fun to start. Enoch especially looked eager, tapping one foot out of rhythm with the stamping and unfolding his arms to flick at his face from time to time in a nervous tic. Despite what Hebron had said he looked like a man who had a bet down on the outcome.

I have no idea how long the dancing and the stamping went on. It couldn't have been as long as it seemed. When it stopped, all at once so that the silence boxed my ears, the two women were wet and gleaming and their sheets were plastered to their flesh, showing their nipples, navels, and pubic mounds as clearly as if they were naked. Their heavy breathing was the only sound in a room that rang with silence like the inside of a great bell.

I didn't let them distract me. I had eyes only for Babel, who sank into a crouch the instant the stamping stopped. That was my signal; I charged him, intending to catch him off balance. But a stone wall is always balanced, and he didn't budge an inch as I hit him with all my weight behind my right shoulder. His long arms closed around me in a bear hug that would have ended the fight there and then if I didn't bend my knees and duck out from under, driving my bootheel into his bare instep as I backpedaled.

That part of the foot is one of the four or five most painful places you can hit a man, but he showed no reaction. Instead, he lunged and backhanded me with a long sweep of his right arm. His knuckles struck the right side of my head like a tree limb; a blue-white light burst inside my skull, and I went down on one knee. He was still coming and I hung on to enough sense to throw myself to the side and roll and come up outside his tremendous reach.

He had fast reflexes for a man his size; for a man of any size. He pivoted just as I let go with a right that I had brought up with me from the floor, shifting his chin so that my knuckles raked his jaw without making square contact. I was still dizzy from the blow to the head, and off balance. He stepped aside, something struck me in the small of my back, and I sprawled headlong to the floor.

I had reason then to thank Hope Weathersill, the madwoman on the Saskatchewan. The buckskin Chief Piapot's Cree had wrapped around my trunk to heal the ribs the woman's bullet had broken had dried as hard as boilerplate. Babel's kick to my back might have cracked my spine if I hadn't still been wearing it. When I scrambled to my feet and turned to meet him again, he was hopping around in a limping circle, trying to walk off the pain of a broken toe. I butted him in the sternum, hard enough to sprain my neck and knock the wind out of a man of normal proportions and take him off his feet. Babel, however, just backed up a step. But it was enough for me to throw both arms around him and snap my head up hard under his chin, colliding with a crack I felt all the way to the ground.

Once again I backpedaled before he could close his arms around me. He blinked, shook his head, spat out a tooth, and went into a fighter's crouch, rocking on the balls of his feet with his big, half-closed fists out in front of him. He knew something of the science of boxing, which made him as dangerous as any man or beast this side of a bull elephant. I feinted with my right, then ducked left, his own left whistling past my ear. I jabbed with my left, but he blocked it with his right and followed through with a blow that caught me in the chest and paralyzed me to the waist. I scissored my knee up into his crotch, but his was higher than most men's, and the pain wasn't enough to slow down his momentum. His looping left fist had by this time completed its circle and caught me behind the neck. My knees buckled, but the blood returned to my head before I finished falling. I dove between his knees, got my shoulder up into his crotch, and lifted with all my strength.

Log bridges don't lift, stone viaducts don't give. He was rooted there. One of his hands closed around my belt in back and he pulled me out from between his legs and lifted me off my feet and threw me away. I had a sensation of flying, of the whites of eyes as the spectators in my path recognized the danger and got out of my way, and then I piled up against the base of a trestle table stacked against the wall.

This was no ordinary fight in as many ways as I could count. There should have been cheering and shouting, but the great hall might have been empty for all anyone raised his or her voice for Babel or against me. In that gulf of silence I found enough of my wind to stand and turn again just as the big man bore down on me in his closed crouch.

Instinct told me to get out of his way. Brother Hebron's voice in my head was louder. *Babel has long arms. . . . You want to get inside them if you plan to do any damage.*

This time I didn't feint. I stuck my right in his face, and as he moved to block it and swoop his own right around, I ducked underneath inside the circle of his arms and hit him with a combination, left-right-left, treating his head like a light bag. That was when he closed his arms around me and squeezed. I heard the ribs Hope Weathersill had broken giving way again just before my lamp went out.

PART THREE

The Stronghold

21

It is never a good idea, Deputy Marshal Murdock, to take advice from one's enemy."

It seemed when I opened my eyes that this conversation had been going on for a while. I was looking up at the rafters of the great dining hall, and certain numb spots in my back told me I was stretched out atop one of the trestle tables. Something cool and damp touched my face; I turned my head just in time to see Fleurette take away the wet cloth and wring it out over a chipped enamel basin balanced on the edge of the table. I knew without turning my head that Philippe stood on the other side.

I said, "Someone's been talking in his sleep." Taking in air to speak brought needles of pain to my injured side.

"We French are not able tacticians," he said. "It must not be forgotten that Napoleon was Italian. Still, it is no great revelation to determine that the logical direction to take in a fight with a man twice one's size is away from him."

"I'm not prone to argue."

Fleurette laughed at that, proving that she did know some English. She had a light, musical titter.

"Where's Claude?" I asked.

"I sent him for our horses. We are free to go as soon as you are ready to ride."

Fleurette said something, and the two conversed in French for a minute. He put an end to it with a harsh *"Non!"* To me: "You *can* ride, Deputy Marshal Murdock, yes?"

"I can if it's away from here. Are you sure I'm included? I lost the fight."

"You should have asked for an explanation of the rules of combat in Shulamite. It is not necessary that you win, merely that you survive. Evidently that is no small feat where Brother Babel is concerned."

"I had a little help."

"So I see." He knocked a knuckle against the buckskin wrap, and I realized my shirt was spread open to expose it. "One would think you knew what was in store."

"One would be wrong. God must love a fool or there wouldn't be so many of us my age."

"It was not just the hide. Queen Fidelity commanded Babel to stop when you were senseless. I gathered from the excitement that it is very rare for her to take a hand in such matters. You must have made a favorable impression upon her."

"I think she liked my name."

"A formidable woman. It is a shame that she must go to hell."

Fleurette crossed herself, then reapplied the damp cloth to my face. She had a sure and gentle touch. The various rebellions and buffalo hunts in which her man had taken part had made her an expert in tending to the sick and injured.

"How far is Cree Lake from here?" I asked.

"Two days in good weather," Philippe said after a moment. "The Sioux stronghold is there. Many of them rode with Crazy Horse in the Little Big Horn fight. You will find the free African community of Shulamite a place of great warmth and hospitality once you approach the stronghold."

"Hebron says that's where I'll find Bliss and Whitelaw."

"Hebron said you would be wise to step inside the arms of Babel."

"He didn't have any reason to lie to me about Bliss and Whitelaw if he expected Babel to kill me. They're there, all right.

You have your family to look after, so if you'll direct me to the lake I'll say good-bye. You've earned that second double eagle and a share of the reward as well."

"My family and I have nothing to fear from our brothers the Sioux. We will go with you. An American can lose himself in that country for a month."

I made a note to stop at Donalbain's farm on my way home and set the old Scot straight about the Métis.

Against Fleurette's protests in rapid French, I sat up and buttoned my shirt. The pain in my ribs was as bad as it had been the first time they were broken, but I had survived it before, and anyway I was sore all over from the beating I had taken, so I just rolled it into the inventory. With Philippe's assistance I got into my bearskin and we went out. The little snake-faced mustang, the gray, and King Henry were packed and waiting for us at the base of the steps. Brother Babel was holding them.

The big man had his boots on now, along with a heavy canvas coat and his floppy hat. There was a purple swelling along the side of his jaw where my fist had raked it, but aside from that he didn't look any the worse the wear for our fight, any more than a tree whose bark I'd nicked with my initials. When I appeared he showed a wealth of teeth — minus one — as crooked as neglected tombstones in what I took to be a grin of recognition from one combatant to another, although twenty-four hours earlier I might have seen it as a savage challenge. If the scar tissue on his face was any indication, I gathered that it was a rare thing when one of his opponents lived for him to grin at.

The members of the Committee of Public Vigilance were standing nearby. The look on Brother Enoch's gaunt face was no greeting. Gripping his Spencer tightly, he turned to say something to Brother Hebron, who shook his head and stepped forward. He didn't offer his hand.

"I didn't mean to give you bad advice," he said. "It was one thing no one ever tried and I was curious to see what would happen."

"No charge for settling the question," I said.

"Queen Fidelity is resting. She claims to be a hundred and ten, and she looks it, so I'm guessing she needs what she gets. She asked me to give you something." He took a small leather pouch from his coat pocket and held it out.

I accepted it after a moment. It was tied

with a cord and something made a whispery sound inside when I shifted it on my palm. It was barely heavier than air. I started to undo the cord.

"Don't open it. She says you'll waste the magic. It's just old bones. She said they belonged to an eagle her grandfather captured with his bare hands. Apparently you impressed her. She says he was a powerful chief."

"Everybody's grandfather was." But I left the knot alone. "Voodoo?"

"She says it's older than that. The magic belongs to the ancient gods, who died before the white man came. She says it will see you home safe."

"What do *you* say?"

"I say bones are bones and there's nothing saying those couldn't have come from last week's chicken. This is the magic I trust." He drew my Deane-Adams from his belt and held it out butt first. "Your long guns are on your horses."

I inspected the loads in the cylinder and holstered the revolver. "I guess this makes me the first white man to leave Shulamite alive."

"That's just a story the Mounties tell to scare the little Mounties. They wouldn't let this settlement stand five minutes if we went around killing every pale-skinned American we saw."

"What made me a special case?"

"Every now and then I have to throw one to the committee. It was just your bad luck to have come along at the end of a long dry spell."

I lowered my voice. "You want to watch your topknot around Enoch. He's hungry."

"That's why I made him number two man. If I learned anything in the army it's to keep your enemies close."

"Indians don't sneak up on that easy."

"I wasn't talking about Indians." He wasn't smiling.

Philippe gave me a boost into the saddle and I rode out in front with my right side on fire. I didn't look back, and I never saw Shulamite or Brother Hebron again, although I heard a year later he came to a short end when one of his own fellow settlers shot him by accident while they were out hunting meat for the winter. There is close, and there is too close, when you do your measuring by the length of a Spencer's barrel.

22

An hour out of Shulamite, the snow I'd been smelling all day came pouring out of the low clouds like bits of candy from a piñata.

The flakes were big to start, floating like paper and melting with sizzling sounds where they landed on coat sleeves and the backs of gloves. They hung up on our eyelashes and left wet trails behind when they slithered down our faces. As the sun descended and the wind picked up, they became smaller and harder, bits of jagged granite rattling against our standing collars and welting our skin. The wind lifted the snow where it fell and threw it at us in buckets. Philippe gave Claude a hand up behind Fleurette and steered King Henry in close to the mustang to shout into my ear, but the wind snatched away his words at a distance of six inches. He jabbed a finger at a patch of shadow a hundred yards ahead. I nodded energetically and we made for the shadow.

It belonged to a stand of virgin pine, the straight trunks so close together we had to go in single file, Philippe's big dun leading the way. We rode for miles through that dense wood, the wind howling outside as around a stockade, before we found a clearing big enough to make camp. While gathering wood in the thickening dark, I stumbled over something and discovered it was the stone foundation of a cabin, the logs having long since burned or rotted away.

"*Coureur de bois*," said Philippe, once we had built a fire big enough to warm our hands. "One of the first, I should imagine. He must have been the only white man for a thousand miles. Perhaps he died of loneliness."

Fleurette said something.

Her husband nodded. "*Oui, ma petit.* More likely he was eaten by a bear. You see what I mean, Deputy Marshal Murdock, about a man alone?"

"You said an American."

"I intended no offense. You carved North America from the wilderness, killed the Indians and the buffalo and felled the trees to make room for your civilization. Here in Canada we did not conquer the wilderness, merely made our peace with it.

But a truce with a bear is only valid until he hungers again."

" 'Grandmother's land,' the Indians call it," I said. "After Victoria. But it's no place for old ladies."

"My grandmother was a Cree, a fierce, white-haired woman who buried two husbands and once beat a puma to death with a piece of firewood. She would feed and shelter you if you loved her, but she never forgot a wrong, and she never slept. You must never think Canada is asleep, or that she has forgiven you your transgressions. Our *coureur* may have expired peacefully in his bed. It is more likely that he fell down a ravine and broke his neck. It would have been a ravine he had descended a thousand times without slipping and thought as safe as a pasture."

"Tell me about the stronghold."

"It is well named. Ten thousand years ago, the big ice that scooped out Cree Lake pushed a million tons of rock into a tower on its eastern shore. It sits like a lion upon its haunches and can only be scaled from the north, where one side of it was beaten into rubble by storms that would have destroyed our *coureur*'s cabin a hundred times a hundred. That side will be guarded heavily. We will not climb it without the permission of those who live on the crest."

"Tell me about them."

"They are Sioux from America. They came here with Sitting Bull after the Custer fight, as you know, and retreated to the stronghold when Sitting Bull agreed to return. They are led by a man called Wolf Shirt. His sister married Crazy Horse, who Wolf Shirt advised not to give himself up to General Crook. It was wise counsel, as history proved."

"I doubt he's reasonable on the subject of white Americans."

"After Crazy Horse was murdered, his wife starved herself to death at the Red Cloud Agency. Peace with white Americans deprived him of his friend and his sister. He has reason to be unreasonable."

"Well, we sure are popular up here."

Philippe blew through his flute to clear it of lint from his pocket. "*I* like you, Deputy Marshal Murdock. However, I do not run with the herd. The one time I did I got shot."

"Brother Hebron said Wolf Shirt harbors fugitives to make himself a nuisance."

"He was right. The Sioux know they cannot win this war, but they can make winning less pleasant for the victors." He moved his shoulders in a Gallic shrug. "It is a small thing, but it is all your army has left them."

"The Sioux must want something they'll take in trade for Bliss and Whitelaw."

"The Black Hills of Dakota, free of white settlers. And sixty million buffalo." He played the flute.

The storm blew for a week, after which the sun came out and we waited another week for the drifts to melt before we could resume our journey. We finished the bacon and the last of the moose. Claude earned his keep by running down snowshoe hares and bringing them into the clearing at arm's length, kicking and screaming at the ends of their powerful hind legs, for Fleurette to bash in their skulls with a chunk of firewood and then skin and clean and cook them on a spit made from pine branches. For variety I went goose-hunting with the Winchester, and nearly wound up meat myself when what I thought at first was a big muskrat hut sticking up out of a frozen pond raised itself to its full height, streaming water, and I found myself staring face to face at eight and a half feet of grizzly. It was covered with silver-tipped hairs like hoarfrost. Its head, with the hair parted in the middle the way bartenders wore it, was as big as a pig, with the little black eyes glittering alongside the great snout, so like the butt end of a charred log.

Bears are nearsighted, but they can detect movement at a greater distance than most humans can. I froze. If I was lucky it would take me for a tree. It grunted, the noise as loud as gravel shifting at the bottom of a sluice, and raised its snout, the nostrils working. I hoped I was downwind. A .44 Winchester will stop a bear, they say, but the bear doesn't always realize it. Not in time to do the shooter any good. At thirty yards only ten leaps kept us apart. I wasn't sure if I could get off twelve rounds in that time, or whether twelve rounds would do the trick.

I willed myself into a pile of rock. A magpie could have landed on me and plucked out an eye and I wouldn't have budged. An eye is a fair trade for not being eaten. The patch and the story would keep me in free drinks for the rest of my life.

The grizzly wasn't any more sure of me than I was. If it thought I was another bear in my coat, it might challenge me for the fishing hole, or go off and look for some less populated spot. It made a test roar: a ripping, rending sound like someone tearing corrugated iron with a wrecking bar. It made every hair on my body stand out, but I didn't move. When it lowered itself I thought it was getting ready to charge. Instead it slapped at the water with a paw the size of a kitchen table, splashing water out over the edges of the jagged hole and onto the ice. Still I didn't react. The bear grunted again and sat back on its haunches, sinking into its rolls of fat and fur in an attitude of frustrated contemplation. It did everything but scratch its head.

It sat there a long time, although nowhere nearly as long as it seemed. I second-thought my plan. If I could shoot it where it sat; but I couldn't will myself to raise the carbine and trigger an attack. I could make a run for it, climb a tree. This time ignorance held me. I couldn't remember if it was a black bear or a grizzly that could climb trees like water rushing up a straw.

And I wondered why in hell this brute wasn't hibernating with all the rest of the bears.

All of which helped to pass the time while the grizzly got tired of waiting. It raised itself again, cuffed the air with a set of claws like railroad spikes, roared again, then shifted its fifteen hundred pounds or so of fur and fat and muscle and short temper onto its forefeet and turned around and mounted the bank on the other side of the pond. It shook itself, water radiating everywhere in lances, and looked back at me over its shoulder one last time, just in case I'd moved or grown a moustache or done something else to make myself look edible. Then it swiveled its head back around and moved off into the trees, making no more noise than a drawer sliding shut.

I held my position, and my breath, for another minute. I didn't want to repeat the episode of the returning moose. Then I heard a crashing back in the underbrush, the bear picking up speed as it went in search of less complicated prey. I let the barrel of the Winchester droop finally. My shoulders ached and the muscles in my jaw felt as if I'd been chewing rawhide for an hour. My clothes beneath the bearskin were drenched. I couldn't have been wetter if I'd swum across the pond. The chill set in then and I turned back toward camp. I completely ignored a goose that exploded from the ground ten feet in front of me and flew in a long rainbow loop down to the hole in the ice the bear had made. I had lost my taste for meat.

I found Philippe clawing the tangles out

of King Henry's shaggy coat with a curry comb and told him about the bear.

"You disappoint me, Deputy Marshal Murdock. A bear steak is worth ten rabbits for stamina on a hard trail. The heart will take you as far as Siberia."

"It was more a question of how far that bear could travel on a Murdock steak."

"You are armed."

"So was he."

"You are sure it was a grizzly?"

"It was big and hairy and a swipe of one of its paws would have sent my head into camp ahead of the rest of me. I didn't ask for further identification."

"Up here the black bear grow nearly as big. Some of the older ones are tipped with silver, as well. One way to make certain is to anger him and then climb a tree. If he climbs up after you, he's a black. The grizzly will merely wait with the patience of Saint Anne for you to come down and be eaten."

"I wasn't that curious."

"You disappoint me," he said again. "I was told all you American frontiersmen shit bear and keep puma for pets."

"That was Jim Bridger. He died last year of a goiter."

"You should have brought the marvelous

Evans rifle. Even if you did not kill him the weight of the lead would have slowed him down so you could walk up to him and cut off a steak for your friend Philippe."

"I went out after geese. I didn't think I'd need eighteen rounds to bring down a gander. Do you want to talk about that bear all day?"

"I did not introduce the subject." He slapped the big dun on the neck and got a purring snort in reply. Then he slipped the comb into the kit at his feet and stretched the kinks out of his small frame. Currying was strenous work; he'd chucked his coat and rolled up his sleeves to expose muscles in his arms as big as train couplings. "How were the drifts?"

"Down," I said.

"Good. We will leave for the stronghold at first light."

The sun was well up when we cleared the woods at last and squinched up our eyes against a plain of white as bright as a salt flat. The trees stood out like embroidery on a sheet, and the sky was bottle-blue and just as clear. A bald eagle had it all to itself, flapping its wings dreamily between updrafts, where it rode the air like a kite. I thought of the eagle bones in the leather pouch in my pocket and hoped they were genuine. It wasn't country for chickens.

"Monsieur le depute!" Philippe's whisper was a harsh rasp, accompanied by his upraised hand.

I heard nothing but the wind in the pines behind us; but the ears of the Métis were as sharp as a deer's. I drew rein.

Fleurette removed her arms from around her husband and craned her neck, pointing her sharp features to the sky as if to smell the air. Young Claude, who had been walking behind King Henry to avoid wallowing in snow to his waist, leaned out to see past the big dun, fixing his bright eyes on what appeared to be an empty space of ground some three hundred yards from where we were waiting. I felt blind and deaf.

The landscape was deceptive. It was not as flat as it seemed under its blanket of snow, which masked long deep depressions gouged by glaciers, like the troughs between waves at sea. As we waited amid clouds of steam from our horses, I heard the first silvery tinkles and flatulent leathery creaks that Philippe had been hearing for minutes, and the others had heard before me. The sounds chilled me to the marrow. In a magnesium flash I was transported back to Murfreesboro, where I had waited with a small patrol in a stand of hickory, covering our mounts' muzzles with our hands to keep them from wickering while Braxton Bragg's Confederate cavalry passed by within pistol range.

The nearest trough shallowed out where Claude was watching. I caught a glint of sunlight off burnished steel, then the brown head and neck of a horse whose coat gleamed like a well-polished boot, and then in a burst like a flock of cardinals, the bright red tunics and brass buttons and spiked white cork helmets of the North-West Mounted Police drawing a brilliant slash four abreast and a quarter of a mile long against the stark white countryside. The Mounties had come to the stronghold.

23

Companyyyyyyyyyyyyyyyyyyy . . . Ulp!"
The master sergeant who bawled the
order had been in the military twenty
years, minimum; a figure arrived at by
assigning a year to each *y* in *company* and
adding three for the total incomprehensi-
bility of his pronunciation of *Halt.* When
their commands could no longer be understood by anyone they were forced into
retirement.

It was the same sergeant with black handlebars I'd seen on the Saskatchewan. He
relayed the order as reluctantly as he'd put
away his side arm when Inspector Urban
Vivian identified me as an ally and not an
enemy come to ambush four hundred
Mounties with a force of two men, a
woman, and a boy. The command was
repeated a couple of times farther back,
and with a racket of creaking saddles, jingling bit chains, snorting horses, and rattling rifle stocks, the column came to a
stop. A warm vapor of perspiration and

spent breath drifted forward and settled over Philippe, Fleurette, Claude, and me like a mist of rain. Then there was eardrum-battering silence.

Vivian broke it. Weeks of riding with the sun slamming off the snow had burned his face as dark as the chestnut he rode and bleached his hair and brush moustache as white as his helmet and belt. His pale eyes stood out like newly minted coins.

"I gave you up for bear bait long ago," he said.

He didn't know how close he'd come to guessing right, but I didn't give him the point. "In Montana we use bears to catch buffalo. I've been taking in the scenery."

"Who is that with you?"

I introduced the du la Rochelles. Vivian surprised me by unstrapping and removing his helmet to nod at Fleurette. His hair, darker on top, had grown out at the temples. He put the helmet back on to address Philippe. "I know you, I think. We have you down as an insurgent."

"Your information is out of date, *monsieur l'inspecteur.* I fight no one these days."

"What brings you this far north?"

I said, "I hired him as my guide."

"He must not be very good. I've been to

Chipewyan and back, and this is as far as you've got."

"We liked Shulamite too much to leave. Then a blizzard hit."

One eye twitched. It was as much surprise as he would show in front of his command. "I don't believe you. Shulamite? You're a liar."

"I'd throw down my glove, but I need it." I let my gaze wander down the line of horsemen. "Every time I see you, you've got a bigger army. Another week or two of Bliss and Whitelaw on the loose and you'll strip the queen of her palace guard."

"That Métis family they butchered up north had a house guest the night they visited. The guest was a priest. If we don't get them first the Métis will do it for us, and burn down every square mile they pass through on the way. This isn't your fight any longer, Murdock. Canada has the greater claim."

I took another look at the column. It was as good a light-horse cavalry as the continent had, if you didn't count the Comanche and northern Cheyenne. In nearly ten years fighting renegades and settling disputes, the North-West Mounted had lost just four men, as opposed to Custer's two hundred during one day's fighting in southern Montana. If I ever wanted to turn over a manhunt to someone else, I wouldn't find a better candidate.

"I'll go home if you'll put it in writing that Judge Blackthorne's court gets Bliss and Whitelaw when you're through trying them."

"I can give you my word to that, as an officer and a gentleman."

"I believe you, Inspector, but if you take a bullet to the head, your word won't be worth one cent more than your brains. I'll need it on paper."

He flushed beneath the sunburn. "Damn it, man, I haven't writing materials to hand."

"Then I'll just ride along with you."

"I can't offer you safe passage. You might think about that before you drag along a woman and a boy. We are on our way to parley with a band of Sioux."

"Wolf Shirt. I got that much from Brother Hebron."

Vivian recognized the names. His nose was running in the cold; he flicked a drop off the end with a white-gloved finger. No one before had ever made so elegant a gesture of it. "Perhaps you were telling the truth about Shulamite. I ask your pardon."

That surprised and irritated me. Most of the fun I'd had in Canada so far, after the weather and renegade slaves and madwomen, was hating Inspector Vivian. "I've been called worse than a liar, and earned some of it," I said. "What's your plan? From what I've heard about Wolf Shirt, he won't give up Bliss and Whitelaw for a sack of beads."

"That's how you Americans handle it. That's how he and his people came to be up here in the first place." Having thus reestablished our animosity, he said, "I intend to appeal to his common sense. Up until now the Sioux have enjoyed the hospitality of the authorities in Canada and sanctuary against prosecution for their differences with the United States of America. If he insists upon harboring fugitives from Canadian law, he sacrifices everything. We have warrants for the arrest of Bliss, Whitelaw, and their companions, and we shall serve them if it means war with the entire Sioux Nation."

"Now you're beginning to sound like Phil Sheridan."

He turned to the man with the black handlebars. "Sergeant Major. Walk-march-trot."

"*Wukmutchtut!*" bawled the other.

262

The column started forward. I turned the mustang's head and gave the lead line a flip to clear the path. Philippe backed King Henry out of the way.

"Indians are muleheaded," I called out above the noise. "They can't count, or they won't. They'll go to war with the rest of the world rather than back off from a position."

"Then they have something in common with Great Britain," he called back over his shoulder.

Philippe and I watched the Mounties pass with our arms folded on our pommels. "What scares me is he thinks that's a good thing," I said.

"It is the same with buffalo," said the Métis. "That's why there are so few left."

We watched the scarlet column trot past, their mounts' hooves churning clouds of powdery snow. Rattling at the rear was a sight that never failed to chill my blood: A pair of men driving a reinforced wagon with the brass bunched barrels of a Gatling gun mounted on a tripod poking out the end of a canvas tarpaulin.

Philippe took in his breath sharply. "A machine for killing," he said. "It is a great time in which we live."

Fleurette, looking confused, leaned forward and said something to her husband, who responded briefly in French. She sat back, crossed herself, then looked around for Claude, who had slid down from behind her. When she spotted him she called his name shrilly. Startled, he scampered over and was caught in a maternal headlock.

I got out my leather pouch and placed two double eagles in Philippe's palm. "The extra is for Shulamite," I said. "I'm pretty sure Brother Enoch was in favor of killing all three of you for riding with me. You didn't have to wait around to watch the fight after the committee said you could go."

He didn't close his hand. "The job is not finished, Deputy Marshal Murdock."

"I hired you to guide me. If I can't follow four hundred Mounties and their eggbeater on wheels from here, I'm no kind of a manhunter. Go home and shoot buffalo."

Fleurette asked another question. When Philippe translated what I'd said, she shook her head, let go of Claude, scooped the gold coins out of her husband's hand, and thrust them toward me.

"She says you hired me to take you to Fort Chipewyan," he said. "Since that is no longer necessary, we will accompany you the rest of the way to the stronghold."

"She didn't say anything."

He showed me his gold teeth. "We have been married a long time, Deputy Marshal Murdock. We do not always have to speak to say what we are thinking."

I took back the eagles. There is no arguing with a woman in any language.

24

French blood leads to exaggeration, and I was prepared to find the Sioux stronghold at Cree Lake a good deal less formidable than Philippe had described it. A half-day short of the lake, however, I saw the broken granite peak of the formation sticking up above the towering white pines that separated us, as straight and tall and imposing as any of the multi-story buildings that were going up in Chicago for the greater glory of the meat barons whose slaughterhouses butchered western beef for New York and London and Paris and a hundred other cities whose residents had never seen a cow any other way but cut up and packaged for sale: *Skyscrapers,* they called them; but the name had never seemed so appropriate as when one applied it to the present feature. When Wolf Shirt and his followers first set eyes upon it, they would have given thanks to the Wise One Above for his sacred gift to Custer's conquerors. I had to think there was something to that, or the Last Stand would have taken place somewhere more defensible than that pimple of a hill on the Little Big Horn.

The Mounties reformed into a column of twos to slice through the girdle of forest that surrounded the lake, sending a cloud of gray squirrels scampering to the tops of the pines to chatter at them from the safe distance of a hundred feet. The du la Rochelles and I got the worst of that; they came down to perch on the branches just above our heads and harangue our tiny group with jabbers and bombardments of pinecones. Claude, riding behind his mother, shocked them into temporary silence when he stood up on the back of the saddle, snatched one off a bough by its tail, and hurled it to the ground, all in one motion. Helena had a baseball team that could have used him at first base.

A rifle cracked when we were still in the woods. No shots followed it, and I concluded that the report was a warning signal fired by a lookout atop the rocks to alert the others to the presence of Mounties. A few minutes later we were clear of the trees and in full view of the lake, broad and flat and painfully blue with white all around, dotted with green scrub and with the red uniforms spreading out to form a straight line between the shore and the forest like a bloody finger drawn across the bottom of a sketch done in colored chalk. Directly across the lake stood the stronghold, a vertical gray cliff thrust like a spear into the level ground, waiting for its gigantic owner to pull it back out and shake loose the trees and shrubbery that clung like moss to the irregularities on its face. It looked twice as tall as it was because nothing separated the base from its reflection on the surface of the water.

The machinery of the cavalry formation was still in motion, the horsemen riding into position to right and left of the center where the inspector and his sergeant major sat as still as the rock itself, the topkick now with his saber unsheathed and resting on his right shoulder after the fashion of a standard. The men in charge of the wagon had drawn it up behind them, and now one was unhitching the team while his partner mounted the bed to remove the tarp from the Gatling. I knew the maneuver that would follow, if reason failed; whether the Indians knew it as well and acted upon that knowledge would make the difference between just a lot of impressive noise and a slaughter.

I handed Philippe the packhorse's lead,

told him and the others to stay where they were, and cantered up to join Vivian. He looked at me out of the corner of one pale eye without turning his head. "Sergeant Major, divest this civilian of his rifles."

"Suh!" said the other, gripped his pommel to swing down. I clapped the muzzle of the Deane-Adams to the bridge of his nose. The front sight barely cleared the lip of his helmet. His eyes crossed comically.

Something triple-clicked in my left ear. I didn't turn my head Vivian's way.

"Murdock," he said.

I said, "I don't want to go to war with Canada, but if I'm going to die anyway I'd just as soon be written about as the man who started it."

A light wind combed the surface of the lake. The inspector let down his hammer gently and holstered his side arm.

"Cancel that order," he said.

I pointed the Deane-Adams skyward and seated the hammer. The sergeant settled back into his saddle and breathed.

Vivian said, "The last time I allowed a civilian to retain his weapons during a parley, he winged a tree-cutter over a boundary dispute. Another lumberman shot back and my French interpreter lost a leg."

"I haven't been a civilian since First Manassas." I leathered the five-shot. "I'll promise not to pot an Indian or a desperado if you'll put the canvas back on that chattergun. I've got sensitive ears."

His face was unreadable beneath the helmet. With the visor covering his brow and the strap buckled at the point of his chin he showed all the individuality of a lead soldier. Finally his gaze shifted toward the sergeant.

"Tell those men to recover the Gatling."

While that was being done I asked Vivian his plan.

"Wolf Shirt affects an ignorance of English, though I suspect he could hold his own in conversation with an Oxford don. However, Indians are muleheaded, as you say, and humoring them takes less time than argument. Corporal Barrymore here is an adept at sign language." He tilted his head an eighth of an inch toward a mass of freckles and sparse red side whiskers mounted at his left. "He will interpret while I determine whether Bliss and Whitelaw and their companions are with the Sioux. If that's the case I have every hope he'll agree with the very good reasons I'll propose for giving them up."

"What makes you think he'll even

agree to talk to you?"

"I have four hundred men and he has sixty."

"And a rock," I said. "Don't forget the rock. He can take target practice on your four hundred redcoats all day while you kick up stone dust."

"I doubt he has the ammunition to withstand a long siege. When he runs out we'll go in and arrest him and hang him in Ottawa if he's killed one trooper or one hundred."

"Now you're talking like an American."

He said nothing, although the muscles of his jaw stood out like doorknobs.

The sergeant major returned then. Vivian tugged a square yard of white handkerchief out of his left sleeve and passed it across the neck of my horse for the other man to take. The sergeant tied it to the end of his saber and trotted up to the edge of the lake with the hilt propped on one thigh, the wind snapping the banner.

A ball of gray smoke appeared in a cleft in the tower of rock near the crest and tore apart in the wind. I heard the crack just as something plopped into the water two feet in front of the sergeant's horse. It wasn't a frog. Man and mount remained motionless, an impressive feat on both counts.

"A warning, I should think," the inspector said.

I said, "Maybe not. I never saw an Indian who was as good with a rifle as he was with a bow."

There were no more shots from the summit, but neither was there anything else for what seemed an hour. Then something white showed in the cleft. It waggled back and forth.

"Right. Sergeant Major, Corporal Barrymore, come with me. Lieutenant Ponsoby, you're in charge. If we're not back by sundown, open fire. Use the Gatling."

"Yes, sir!" This from a youth with a hooked nose and an undershot jaw like a monkey wrench. When his teeth went, the one would touch the other. He'd be a general by then, if one of his own men didn't shoot him first.

I spurred the mustang into line behind the others. Vivian glared back once over his shoulder but said nothing. Evidently he'd decided that humoring me took less time than arguing.

Philippe's information about the configuration of the rock proved correct. The north face bore little resemblance to the south, having collapsed into a pile of broken shards, boulders the size of the courthouse in Helena, and round stones no larger than a man's fist. It had all happened long enough ago for scrub pine and thistles to have grown from the soil deposited in the cracks. The way was not fit for horses, and so we tethered ours and began scaling on foot, the sergeant leading the way with the flag of truce.

It was warm climbing. The wind had sculpted a horseshoe-shaped concavity in the snow east of the lake, and the sun coming off that white dish had made the rocks hot to the touch; at high noon a man could have fried bacon on one of them. Grasping stones and twisted tree trunks for leverage, I kept an eye on the cracks for rattlesnakes. I had no idea if they grew them this far north, but it was an old habit in that kind of landscape. I was sweating and wanted to ditch the bearskin; the wind whistling up near the crest warned me to hold onto it. The mountain country back home was scattered with the bones of trappers and Indian traders who had abandoned their winter gear to avoid heat stroke and frozen to death a few hours later.

Twenty yards from the top the route became almost vertical. The sergeant tore loose his white handkerchief and scabbarded his saber to free both hands for climbing. Corporal Barrymore, following him, put his foot on a ledge of rock that turned out to be rotten and saved himself from falling by grabbing a handful of dense moss. Meanwhile Vivian and I flattened out against the cliff while a bucketful of rubble, twigs, and coarse earth bounced off our hats and shoulders and went down inside our collars. Then we resumed climbing with the grit rubbing our joints.

When we stood on the crest at last I was rewarded for hanging onto the bearskin. The wind was stiff and steel-cold and made my face numb. I had removed my gloves for climbing. Now I got them out of a pocket and wriggled into them. My fingers were already stiffening. The Mounties retrieved their white gauntlets from their belts and put them on.

I caught a glimpse of the lake below and the red tunics of the North-West Mounted, strung out like bright ribbons on white linen.

"Well, Charlie, look what we have here. Three red kings and a black jack. I'd call it a misdeal."

The man who spoke was short and thick and held a rifle braced against his right hip. He was standing against bright sky, which made his face a purple blur. His companion, with a spire of rock behind him, was easier to make out: slender, almost frail looking, with a round face that appeared to have been nailed to the wrong body. His skin was the color of raw iron ore, against which the whites of his eyes stood out and his long canine teeth when he smiled, as he did now. I recognized him from wire descriptions as Charlie Whitelaw, the Cherokee killer from the Indian Nations. That made his friend with the rifle Lorenzo Bliss.

25

I reckoned I was the black jack, because of the bearskin. It gave me leave to open.

"You boys should have kept traveling. You're hemmed in tight up here."

Bliss took two steps my way and swung the rifle, laying the barrel alongside my left temple. I stumbled, but I'd been anticipating something along those lines and was moving in the same direction when the blow came. I kept my feet while the black tide went out.

He was as fast with a rifle as he was said to be with a knife. Vivian's hand was still going down for his side arm when the long gun came back around and Bliss levered a shell into the chamber. As he did so a perfectly good unfired cartridge spat out of the ejector and rolled to a stop in a crevice at his feet. That told me two things about him: 1. He was wasteful; 2. He had a weakness for making dramatic gestures. I banked the information for whatever good it might do me.

"Finish what you started," he told the inspector. "I been wanting to find out if you can see blood on them pretty red blouses."

Vivian spread his arms away from his sides.

Whitelaw said, "If you're going to throw away good ammo, toss me that gun."

I could see Bliss's face now that he was standing closer. It was all Irish except for the eyes. He had a pug nose and a long upper lip with an oddly delicate dimple, visible through his sparse, sun-bleached moustaches, that would make him appear boyish even in old age — a waste, considering his chances of getting that far. His eyes were black and Spanish. They were the humorless eyes of his prostitute mother looking out through the holes in a comic mask.

Without hesitating he threw the rifle to Whitelaw, who caught it and pulled down on us before we could react. It was a Henry, the full-length .44 with a brass receiver and a folding sight. In the same movement, Bliss scooped a huge bowie knife from the scabbard on his belt and turned it to catch the light on its oiled blade. I wondered if it was the same one he'd used to cut out a man's heart in a saloon in Wyoming.

Whitelaw said, "Take their weapons."

With a show of reluctance, Bliss scabbarded the knife and stepped forward to relieve us of our side arms and the sergeant of his saber. He tossed them onto a patch of soft earth hammocked in a hollow at the base of a boulder. When he paused to sneer at my English revolver, I got a strong whiff of sweat and fermented grain. The whiskey seemed to be leaking directly out of his pores, as if his body were saturated with it and could hold no more. For all that he was steady on his feet and there was no slurring in his speech. Men who drink constantly build up an immunity to drunkenness right up until their livers explode.

"Skinny little pistol for a man," he said. "I bet you squat to make water."

"I bet you'd watch."

His grin, split catlike by the deep dimple in his upper lip, fled. He fisted the Deane-Adams and I braced myself for another blow. But Whitelaw barked at him and he spat on the pistol instead and threw it onto the pile, hard enough to nick the metal.

That took the edge off. He stared at me from a distance of two feet, the grin working its way back. He brought up his right hand, slid his index finger across the underside of my jaw in a slow cutting motion, pursed his lips at me, and stepped away.

I stopped worrying then. John Swingtree had told me back in the penitentiary at Deer Lodge that Charlie Whitelaw did all the thinking for the pair, and it had taken me two minutes in their company to confirm that. Bliss was the one to keep an eye on — there was no connection between his brain and his hands, and even he couldn't predict what he'd do or when he'd do it — but Whitelaw was the one to outsmart. He'd have everything figured three moves ahead.

They are hell together, Swingtree had said. *They wasn't nothing till they met, just a couple of bad hats rolling along, waiting for somebody to stomp 'em flat. Split them up and that's what will happen. . . .*

He also said I'd get myself killed trying to split them up. But you can't believe everything a half-breed tells you, and a convict into the bargain.

"My name is Urban Vivian. I'm an inspector with the North-West Mounted Police. I've come to speak with Wolf Shirt, the Sioux chief. Where is he?"

Whitelaw smiled at the Englishman,

showing his canines. "I'll introduce you."
He stepped sideways and made a motion
with the rifle.

A well-trod path led through a cleft in
the rocks into a circular enclosure surrounded by granite, as if an enormous
spoon had scooped a piece out of the top
of the rock. It was a couple of acres, big
enough to erect some lodges and build a
community fire, which still crackled inside
a circle of stones. There were no lodges,
however; a number of distinctive hoop-
shaped depressions in the dust showed
where some had stood until recently, but
there was no other sign of habitation.
When we stepped into the area, Bliss and
Whitelaw following, we shared it with a
dozen white men in overcoats and an
Indian woman seated cross-legged on the
ground beside something stretched out on
a buffalo robe. The woman was wailing
softly, a sound that until that moment I
had taken for the wind moaning through
openings in the rock.

The men were loaded down heavily with
cartridge belts, belly guns, and rifles, but I
didn't need any of that to conclude that
this was the gang that had raped its way
across four territories and the Dominion of
Canada over a period of eighteen months.

Men who had been traveling and living together for a long time tended to look alike, after the fashion of stones rolled along a riverbed or more precisely a pack of mongrels; worn by constant movement and shared instinct to the same shape, color, and texture, gaunt and brown and sandy-looking, slit-eyed and jerk-jointed, with whatever humanity they might have started out with strung out in the bends and snags and cataracts upstream. Two of them were Negroes, and another was twice as old as the average, with a bad eye and dull white moustaches like dirty linen, but for that they might have all belonged to the same unnatural litter. They watched us with the steady naked intensity of scavengers standing around a shared carcass.

The woman on the ground looked sixty. She could as easily have been forty; it was a brutal life, for all the eastern writers made of its simple nobility. Her hair was unfettered and streaked with broad bands of leaden gray, her doeskin dress torn away from one shoulder, exposing nearly all of one breast. She sat with her palms turned upward on her knees. I took the three diagonal red stripes she wore on each forearm as some kind of tribal marking until I noticed that she was bleeding from them and had been for a long time. Most of the blood had dried brown on her arms, staining her dress and the rock upon which she sat the same rusty color. The keening noise she made was very soft, not because she was trying to be quiet, but because she had been doing it for at least as long as she had been bleeding, and she was exhausted and hoarse. She was mourning.

The buffalo robe she sat beside had been spread carefully, its wrinkles smoothed out from the center toward the edges. Upon it lay the body of an Indian man of about fifty. His iron-gray hair was braided, the braids socketed in cylinders made of otterskin decorated with porcupine quills dyed red and blue. He wore a headdress of white eagle feathers tipped with black and sewn into a beaded band. An intricate breastplate made of small bones, as flexible as chain mail, covered an outfit of soft white skins, the sleeves and leggings trimmed with long fringe. His winter moccasins, decorated with beading and quillwork, extended to his knees. His hands were folded on his chest, and a longbow and lance made of ironwood and an elaborate quiver filled with arrows lay alongside him; he would need them to sustain himself in the well-stocked hunting fields that awaited him beyond this life.

The face beneath the headdress wore a permanent scowl. The skin was cracked all over like dried mud and the deep lines that framed the corners of the wide mouth might have been scored with a knife. The flesh had already begun to shrink in the intense sunlight.

Corporal Barrymore crossed himself. The sergeant turned his head and spat over his left shoulder. They would belong to different denominations.

Vivian looked down at the corpse without expression. "Wolf Shirt?"

"That's what his woman said." Whitelaw's canines clenched his lower lip like fangs. "We didn't kill him. He died all on his own before we got here."

"Where are the others?" I asked.

"Cleared out. The chief was the only thing keeping them from going back south and turning theirselves in to the army."

"Injuns are dumb as cowflop," Bliss said.

Whitelaw said, "I'm Indian."

"You wasn't brought up in a leather house with your ass hanging out of a washrag."

"Ballocks." The sergeant wiped the spittle from his moustache with the back of a hand. "They wouldn't run off and leave their chief's squaw out here in the open without provisions."

"They would if no one volunteered to take her in," I said. "Not many do. It's hard enough looking after one's own woman and children with the buffalo gone."

"Savages," said the corporal.

I shook my head. "Just different. Forgotten people starve to death in alleys back East every day."

"They should of held out," said Bliss. "Life on a rock beats getting hung in Dakota."

Whitelaw's laugh was a dry cough. "We ought to know."

"Their old people probably want to be buried back home," I said. "Wolf Shirt's death helped them make the decision. Some of their young have never seen the places they tell stories about. If the stories die too it's as if they never lived." I looked at the outlaws. "What I'd like to know is how you got the woman to tell you anything. They don't stop to talk when they're mourning their dead."

Bliss made that grin that gave out short of his eyes. "It wasn't her first choice. Charlie signed to her I'd cut off her man's business and throw it off the rock if she didn't answer some questions. Injuns got a thing against facing their maker without all the parts he sent them down with in the first place."

"You should have moved on," Vivian said. "Now you're trapped."

Bliss said, "We *was* trapped. Now we got us a Pullman ticket out."

"We're going to play those three red kings, misdeal or no," Whitelaw said. "You redbirds have got this far without losing too many feathers. I'm thinking your men will clear us a path if they don't want to lose three in one shot."

"A path to where?" I asked. "You're wanted in two countries now."

The Cherokee turned his round face my direction. "Talk some more."

"And say what? I'd read the Bible if I had one and I thought it would take."

"You're American," he said. "What you doing so far off your range?"

"Chasing you."

"Law?"

"I'm a deputy U.S. marshal."

"Well, we can't use you. Stick him, Lolo. Cut his heart out."

Bliss was moving almost before White-law spoke. He had his bowie in his right hand as he lunged and I turned right to narrow the target, but it was just a feint. He border-shifted the knife to his left and drove in low and hard to come up under my ribcage, and I wasn't fast enough in this world or the next to protect myself.

He was as strong as a bull; I felt the blow to my teeth and my cracked ribs pulled apart and snapped back together, pinching me so that for an instant I thought it was the knife going in. But the buckskin wrap that still encased my torso was as hard as oak. I saw the surprise in his face when the blade struck it. Before he could recover I turned inside him, got both hands on the arm holding the knife, brought up my knee, and broke his arm across my raised thigh as if it were a piece of firewood. The knife dropped from his nerveless hand and I shoved him back and bent to scoop it up. Barbs of granite stung my hand and the knife sped away. I didn't even hear the report of the Henry in Whitelaw's hands. When I straightened, rubbing the back of my hand, smoke was still twisting out the end of the barrel.

"Rock breaks scissors," he said.

The rest of the gang had their weapons out and trained on me. I worked my fingers to make sure the tendons were still in operation but didn't move apart from that.

The back of my hand was flecked with blood as if I'd tangled up with barbed wire.

Bliss was half bent over, holding his broken arm against his side. The pain hadn't started yet. "Son of a bitch is wearing some kind of armor!"

"You must of missed and hit his belt buckle," Whitelaw said.

"Horseshit! Make him open his damn shirt."

"I reckon you better open it. Lolo's hard to simmer down once he gets a prickly pear up his ass."

I'd unbuttoned the bearskin for the climb up the rock. Now I unfastened my shirt and spread it apart. The belt of rawhide looked like a dirty plaster cast. It was looser than it had been when it was fresh. I could have shucked it off over my head if my arms didn't get in the way.

"Jesus!" Bliss was shrill. "There's the dent the bowie made. I made deeper cuts in trees."

"That regulation wear for lawmen in Montana these days?" Whitelaw asked.

"My own invention. I thought it might keep me warm." I was gambling on a member of one of the Five Civilized Tribes knowing nothing of Cree medicine. My ribs were still healing from the fight with Brother Babel and I saw nothing good in letting this bunch in on any weaknesses. The smell of blood has the same effect on scavengers everywhere.

Vivian stepped in to my rescue. "You'd better get help for your friend's arm. I heard it break in at least two places."

Whitelaw said, "Well, now, maybe you'd care to fix up a splint. Seeing as how the only wood on this here rock is what's burning in that fire."

"You could file the barrel off that rifle, Luther's got them tools off that blacksmith we kilt in Sheridan." Bliss's voice was getting shallow. The shock was wearing off and the pain was starting.

"I ain't going to saw the barrel off this Henry."

"Roy! You said you trusted your Colt before that Springfield."

"Not past fi'ty feet." The old man spread his moustaches to show six teeth spread out in bunches. He filled his hollow chest as if he were breathing in the other man's pain.

"Laban! Redfoot! You niggers can't hit the obvious side of a buffalo with them long guns."

The two Negroes, a big one with a

scatter of black beard and a small one in a river pilot's cap, shook their heads. They were both grinning broadly.

"You goddamn cunts! Sons of bitches! Cornholers! *Hijos de las putas!*" The rest was Spanish outside my range. It was evidently a far more versatile language for the purpose he had in mind. He was holding his left arm so tight the knuckles of his right hand stood out like white porcelain drawer knobs.

"I do like to listen to Lolo cuss. Just about everything else about him gets on my nerves." Whitelaw covered his canines and poked his rifle at Vivian. "You got some talking to do. Climb up on that tall rock and show your men that pretty red uniform."

"Go to blazes!"

The Cherokee braced the Henry against his hip. Vivian folded his arms across his chest. His expression was the same as the one he had showed me in Moose Jaw when we were discussing the relative merits and deficiencies of the British Empire and the United States of America.

After thirty seconds, Whitelaw breathed in and out quickly, an exasperated sigh, and relaxed his grip on the rifle. Then he swiveled and shot young Barrymore in the chest.

The freckle-faced corporal sat down on the rock and fell over sideways with his legs still spread out in front of him. His white helmet tilted to one side and blood slid out of his mouth into a pool on the rock. It was much darker than his tunic, almost black.

Whitelaw jacked in a fresh shell and pointed the Henry at the sergeant.

"Your party's getting smaller, Inspector. You want to go down with Custer?"

After a moment Vivian uncrossed his arms and started climbing.

26

The inspector braced himself in the same cleft in the rock where the warning shot had been fired into the lake earlier. When it was certain that the Mounties stationed along the shore had recognized the uniform, Whitelaw fed Vivian the words and he bawled them out. He repeated them to make sure nothing was lost, then came down. His face was stiff and flushed beneath the sunburn. It was cold up there and the wind shrilled through the cleft.

"Think it took?" Whitelaw asked him.

"They're taught to obey orders."

You could see the Cherokee thinking. He jerked his chin toward the corporal's corpse. "Strip off that uniform."

"Do it yourself," Vivian said.

"Yours'd fit me just as good." Whitelaw raised the rifle.

Once again the inspector crossed his arms. Whitelaw said shit and motioned with his weapon. "Laban, strip off that uniform."

The big Negro set his feet. "I ain't touching no dead corpse."

"You touched plenty that had a poke in their pockets."

"I didn't take off their damn clo'es."

Redfoot, the small Negro in the pilot's cap, came forward. "I'll do it. I worked for a undertaker one whole summer in McAlester."

Whitelaw blocked his path with the Henry's barrel. "I told Laban to do it."

"I ain't your nigger."

Whitelaw stepped back and aimed low. "I'll blow off your kneecap and you and Lolo can help each other down the rock. You can watch your leg rot down on the flat."

Redfoot said, "Come on, Laban. You can give me a hand with his boots."

Laban stuck it out as long as he could, then moved in to help. Outlaws on the run had a horror of untreated wounds. They'd made their peace with the hangman's rope, but not with gangrene.

I said, "I thought you boys got along better than this. What's kept you glued together?"

"We're O.K. as long as we keep moving. Goddamn it, Lolo, quit your blubbering. You sound worse than the woman."

Bliss was sitting on the ground now with his arm cradled in his lap. His face was the color of unbleached muslin and clammy looking. "Go to hell, you cornholing son of a red squaw bitch." His voice was without tone.

"Yeller, whittle a pair of splints off that lance."

A thick-built party in a buffalo coat and a sail-brimmed hat with a feather in the band left the group and produced a skinning knife from a soft leather sheath on his belt. His beard was bright yellow against the burned brown of his skin. The Indian woman left off wailing as he approached Wolf Shirt's corpse. She was watching him out the corner of one eye. When he bent down to pick up the lance, she launched herself to her feet and fell upon him from behind, twining her legs around his waist and clawing his face with both hands.

She was silent now, saving her energy for breathing and tearing skin. Yeller was making all the noise. He howled and cursed and spun around, trying to throw her off, while Whitelaw and the others — all except Bliss — laughed and shouted encouragement to the woman: "Claw out his eyes!" "Bite his ear!" "Throw him down and squat on his face!" Finally he remembered he was holding a knife. He slashed at her left arm, and he must have cut a tendon because she let go of her grip and she was too weak from loss of blood to hold on with the other. He flung her off and she fell on her back and before she could get up, he bent over her and slashed right and left with long hacking movements of his arm, like a farmer cutting wheat. A lariat of blood unfurled in the air and splattered the toe of my right boot. I stepped forward, but Whitelaw was between us in a stride with the Henry raised and I stopped. My hands hurt. I was making fists so tight my nails cut into my palms.

It was over in three or four seconds. Yeller straightened, breathing heavily and dripping blood from the deep scratches on his face. The woman lay without moving.

"Now cut those splints," Whitelaw said.

Ironwood doesn't cut easily. Yeller worked for an hour at the handle of the lance, cursing under his breath and drawing a sleeve across his face from time to time to clear his eyes of sweat and blood, while Bliss moaned and cursed and rocked back and forth over his shattered arm and Whitelaw tried on the uniform that Laban and Redfoot had removed from Corporal Barrymore. The others played cards with a tattered deck on a saddle blanket spread on the ground, betting gold watches, paper money, and silver forks they'd plundered across the north country. Roy, the old man with the bad eye — it looked like a gob of yellow spittle quivering between his corrugated lids — sat out to guard the prisoners with his Springfield carbine across his lap. We prisoners sat on the ground and conversed in low whispers.

"I promoted Barrymore from the ranks," Vivian said. "I planned to recommend him for officer's training in Ottawa."

The young man lay on his back in his white long-handles, clean except for the stain around the blue hole in his chest. One of his heavy ribbed woolen socks had come off when his boots were removed. His foot was clean and white, like a woman's hands.

The sergeant ground his teeth on his moustaches. "They're a pack of dogs. Hanging's too kind for their like. We ought to bring back drawing and quartering."

I said, "I'll sign the petition. Right now I wouldn't give us until midnight to finish drawing it up before they kill us. They'll wait for dark to move out. That's their best chance to confuse your men with that Mountie uniform. After that they'll put us away to make time."

"Where are their horses?" asked the sergeant.

"This looks like box canyon country," I said. "They'll have them corraled in one and under guard. They'll head there first thing."

Vivian was still thinking about Barrymore. "My fault. Stubborn old regular army officer. That's what's costing us India."

"He's dead," I said. "We're not. If we can get to our horses on the way down we might be able to make the break."

"My fault." Vivian was looking at the ground.

He wasn't going to be any help.

Whitelaw tried tugging on one of the corporal's boots, then gave up and stamped his feet into his old worn stovepipes. The black cavalry trousers with the white stripe up one side were a good fit and the tunic answered, although it was a little long in the sleeves and snug across the chest, where the buttons strained. The helmet was too small but he adjusted the chinstrap and it looked as if it would stay put if he didn't move too hastily. He could have fooled a good eye at some distance and in the dark. If the Mounties shot anyone it wouldn't be him.

Bliss must have been reading my mind. "I need a red suit too. That muckety inspector's getup looks like it might fit."

"You'd never get the coat on over that arm," Whitelaw said. "I ain't just out to save my hide. They sent three of their men up here. If only two come back down they might open fire out of pure orneriness."

"Horseshit. You're a yellow injun."

Whitelaw made one of his long strides and kicked his arm. Bliss made a high-pitched shriek, then rolled over, pinning the arm to his side, and vomited. A sharp stench of half-digested whiskey soured the air. Whitelaw made his dry cough of a laugh and went over to join the card game.

"Thieves' honor." The inspector seemed to have stopped thinking about Barrymore.

"Outlaw fever," I said. "When wolves run together long enough, they start going at each other."

"Drawing and quartering," said the sergeant.

Vivian said, "They'll expect us to go for our horses. They'll send a man ahead to cut them loose."

I said, "Hold them, maybe. Whitelaw will want them close in case anything goes wrong between here and where they're hiding their own mounts. If it comes down to shooting he'll save himself first. Bliss was right about that business of keeping the count. He's betting on that uniform to save his life."

Vivian shook his head. "It's a wonder they stayed together this long."

"They were born to ride partners. No one else but the devil would have them."

"Ghastly country you have, that turns out beasts such as them."

This time I didn't rise to the inspector's lure. If I did, we wouldn't be getting on any better than Whitelaw and Bliss.

Yeller finished the splints finally and cut a dozen long fringes from Wolf Shirt's sleeve to tie them in place on Bliss's arm. Before that he placed his foot against the injured man's chest and jerked back on the arm with both hands to set the bone. If the Mounties down on the flat didn't hear the scream, they must have been paying attention to something else. Bliss passed out after that.

Whitelaw measured the height of the sun with his hands and told Yeller to wrap the chief in the buffalo robe before he began to stink. "Throw the woman and that redbird corporal in with him."

"Tell one of the niggers to do it. Redfoot can paint them pink and stick a lily in their paws." He was sitting on a rock with his greasy hat balanced on its crown in his lap and the sweatband turned inside out to dry, dabbing at his scratches with a filthy blue bandanna wetted down from his canteen. Wispy blonde strands crawled about his naked scalp in the breeze. It was a pale cap above the line where his sunburn left off, white as a grub.

The Henry's stock swung and collided with Yeller's head. He fell off the rock and came up holding his skinning knife. The blade was clotted with gore. He hadn't bothered to clean it before putting it away.

The Cherokee followed him up with the barrel of the rifle. His sharp canines slid out. "You want to run this outfit?" he asked.

Yeller looked at the muzzle but didn't let go of the knife. The whites of his eyes swam with blood.

"I'll make it easy." Whitelaw lowered the rifle from his hip. He sank into a crouch, laid the weapon on the ground, and stood back up. He moved slowly and his eyes never left the other man's. "You want to run this outfit? Tell me what you're fixing to do when you get off this rock."

A gray tongue slid along Yeller's lips and went back inside like a toad. He bounced the knife in his hand, improving his grip. "Make a run for it."

"If you run they'll fire up that chatter-gun and cut you into smaller pieces than you did the woman. You can do better than that. Think with your head, not your feet."

"After I stick you I'll put on that there uniform. They won't shoot one of their own."

"That might work. What about the others, Lolo and Roy and Laban and the rest? There ain't uniforms enough to go around. You need a plan to make them follow you down the rock that won't spare you and kill them. Otherwise you'll never make it down alive."

"You ain't told us *your* plan."

"I never tell you anything you don't need to know. That's got us this far, all of you know that. You're brand new. You got to show them they can trust you to take them through. Come up with anything yet?"

There they were, Whitelaw smiling, showing his sharp teeth with his hands empty, and Yeller holding the knife he'd killed with once that day, looking as if he were the one under the threat. Remington could have painted the picture down to the last detail, caught the glint in the Cherokee's eye and made the beads of sweat glitter on the bald man's head, and nobody would have bought it or risk having to explain the picture to everyone who saw it.

"Well, how do I know you even *got* a plan?" Yeller wanted to know.

"Because God gave me brains, and all He gave you is that little knife. I was you, I'd take better care of it. Your good looks won't get you off this rock."

The others had lost interest in their game. Only Roy, who kept his good eye on us with his carbine across his thighs, wasn't watching. The men's faces were alive with interest, but none of them seemed eager to take a hand or choose sides. They didn't want to wind up on the wrong one. Bliss was either still out or listening quietly. It was anyone's bet which one he'd root for.

"Any luck?" Whitelaw asked. "I don't want to make you nervous, but there's only an hour of daylight left."

"Shit." The bald man with the yellow beard wiped off both sides of the blade on his pants, jammed the knife into its sheath, and turned to look after the corpses.

The air lifted then. The men picked up their cards and resumed making bets. Whitelaw picked up the Henry. He'd stopped smiling.

"Leave off that," he told Yeller. "Laban, Redfoot, wrap up them carcasses. You was right, Yeller. It ain't work for a white man."

Yeller turned back and stared at him a long time before he scooped up his hat and slapped the dust off it and jammed it onto his head with both hands. His face was absolutely empty of intelligence. Mine was too, or I was a better poker player than I thought.

27

The sun slid into a slot in the granite pinnacle on the west side of the stronghold, throwing long fingers of shadow across the two men struggling to drag the bodies of the Indian woman and the Mountie corporal onto the buffalo robe. When they stooped to lift one side of the robe, Lorenzo Bliss stirred himself for the first time in an hour.

"Hang on." Throwing his splinted left arm straight out for balance, he put his right hand on the ground and pushed himself to his knees and then his feet. He found his bowie knife where it had fallen and knelt over the bodies. After a minute he wiped the knife on the robe, sheathed it, and rose, holding a long iron-gray banner in his right hand. I looked down, saw the raw red patch on the front of Wolf Shirt's skull, and directed my gaze to the scuffed toe of my left boot until my stomach walloped to a halt.

"I always wanted a chief's scalp." He held the thing by one end and snapped it several times like a whip to shake off the loose gore. "You know how to tan one of these things, Charlie?"

"Cherokee don't take scalps." Whitelaw buckled on Barrymore's belt.

"I reckon if I soak it in brine and dry it in the sun, it'll keep. I'll get it wove into a belt or something later." He pulled off the kerchief he had tied around his neck and tried wrapping the bloody end in it one-handed, but he was clumsy. Whitelaw took the scalp from him, wound it a few times around one hand, then took the kerchief and tied it into a neat bundle and stuck it into the side pocket of Bliss's canvas coat. "Don't forget and leave it in there if you don't want to stink like a goat."

"Or an injun." Bliss grinned.

"Better an injun than a greaser mick bastard."

They were friends again now.

Bliss sent Yeller to collect the hip guns he'd taken off us. When he returned carrying one in each hand with two more stuck in his belt, Bliss relieved him of my Deane-Adams and came over to where I was sitting on the ground. He cocked the revolver, stuck the barrel under my chin, and lifted it. I saw my reflection in his black eyes.

"What do they call you in Montana?" he asked.

"Murdock."

"Hell, I never heard of you." He raked the sight across the underside of my chin, took the pistol off cock, and shoved the barrel under his belt. "You want it, take it," he said.

I yanked it out and thrust it into his groin in the same motion. I felt his reaction right through it. He'd expected me to think about it first.

Something hard and cold touched my left temple, still tender from the blow earlier: the muzzle of Roy's Springfield.

"You shoot, you die," he said.

I spun the Deane-Adams, offering the handle to Bliss. I managed to loosen my grip before he could tear my hand with the sight the way he had my chin.

"Lolo, if you was any dumber you couldn't bore an asshole in a wood duck," Whitelaw said. "He ain't one of them tin panners on the Saskatchewan."

"Blast him, Roy," Bliss said.

"Back off, Roy. Them Mounties will think we're shooting our prisoners."

Roy backed off.

Bliss leaned his face close to mine. Beads of sweat showed in the delicate cleft in his upper lip. "When I get you down on the ground, I'll gut you like a frog."

I said nothing. He walked away.

"You should have pulled the trigger." The sergeant's voice was a hissing snarl.

Vivian said, "If he had, you'd be sitting with his brains in your lap."

I didn't take part in the discussion. Roy's carbine wasn't the reason I hadn't fired. I never drew a weapon just to make a point. In the natural order of things I'd have emptied the chamber under the hammer as soon as I felt resistance on the other end, before the old man had a chance to throw down on me. If it had been Whitelaw instead of Bliss, or any of the others, I wouldn't have hesitated. One of the things I'd learned from war is that wounding a man causes more trouble for the enemy than killing him outright; if they cared about their own, an injured man took two more out of combat to carry him to safety, and a delay of a few minutes can make the difference in the way a battle comes out. Bliss's arm was already crippled. That meant he'd need help getting down off the rock and making his escape with the others. Dead, he'd be left where he fell to feed whatever did the work of buzzards in Canada, and the rest would be free to flee at their own pace.

Of course, I was counting plenty on Vivian's Mounties being in a position to take advantage of the slowdown — and on Whitelaw and the rest of the gang thinking enough of Lolo to mess with the burden.

In a little while the sun had gathered up the last of its heat and stolen below the edge of the rock. The last yellow flames of the campfire were licking at the crumbs of unburned wood that remained and warmed little but themselves. The first steel clamp of Arctic cold closed around my ears and neck. I turned up the bear-skin's collar and buttoned it to my throat. It chafed the flesh beneath my chin where Bliss had raked it with the Deane-Adams' front site.

The chill made Bliss's arm throb. He paced about to increase his circulation, working the fingers that stuck out as red as radishes between the splints and calling Whitelaw in English and Spanish a whore's son for ever suggesting they leave the Nations for this frozen shitpile in the middle of no place. The fact that Bliss's own mother was a whore didn't seem to enter into the logic of the moment. The Cherokee paid him no attention. He was busy drilling the others on what he expected of them when he gave the order to pull out. Corporal Barrymore's uniform had begun to have its effect upon his tone and bearing — and on the way Laban and Redfoot and Roy and Yeller and the rest nodded assent. In all that murdering crew there was not one word said in interruption. Brass and bright colors were much easier to make sport of at a distance than close up and when your immediate future depended upon who was wearing it. Beneath that lay the understanding that Whitelaw and Bliss had taken them this far, with hundreds of peace officers in two countries wearing out horseflesh and telegraph wires to capture them and stretch their necks. These men would have laughed to read the superhuman stuff that was written about the pair in the eastern dreadfuls, but they would not have discounted it as impossible.

It was nearly dark now in that high hollow circle of weathered and broken stones, but there was still plenty of light on the flat. We were waiting for the darkness to reach the ground. A lantern was lit so Roy could keep an eye on us prisoners, but the wick was turned low to preserve the gang's night vision. The coal-oil fumes mingled with the lingering sulphur stink of spent powder and the stench of butchering, and might have made me retch if I had anything in my stomach. I realized then how many hours had passed since I'd eaten. My stomach rumbled.

The top layer of purple turned dirty-brown over the western territories, then disappeared beneath the black. There was no moon, but the snow provided its own illumination, with the lake a tattered black oval in the white. A pie-faced youth the others called Stote, with a downy froth of whiskers and nails gnawed down to bleeding stumps, produced a grubby almanack, moved his lips over it in the light from the lantern, and announced they had an hour before the rise of the quarter moon. Whitelaw's instructions kicked in then. Vivian, the sergeant, and I were told to stand up and herded through the cleft to the ledge where Bliss and Whitelaw had first thrown down on us. There, armed with the lantern and his Springfield, Roy held us at bay while the two Negroes went over the edge and Yeller tied a rope from his kit around Bliss's chest under his arms. Then Stote and a man with yellow-brown eyes like a wolf's helped Bliss over the edge and lowered him, grunting advice and curses, to where Laban and Redfoot waited to receive him where the descent relaxed into a gentle grade. The process must have been agonizing for Bliss, but he bore it in silence, probably with teeth clenched; any complaint would have carried down to the lake and given the Mounties too much time to think. I caught a glimpse of him on the way down, dangling with his splinted arm stuck out to the side like a damaged wing, and remembered the too many men I had seen hanged. And I wondered if he was in too much pain to ask himself if this was what he had to look forward to.

When he was safely down and untied, Stote and the wolf-eyed man made the end of the rope fast to a rock for the rest to clamber down. Yeller, who had rescued Wolf Shirt's longbow from the buffalo robe, passed it down for Bliss to use as an alpenstock to steady himself during the walk down, then used the rope to lower himself hand over hand. The others, all except Roy and Whitelaw, followed him; then Whitelaw fixed the Henry over his shoulder by its sling and made the descent somewhat clumsily; a century of the white man's brand of civilization had leeched away most of the survival skills of his Cherokee ancestors.

Then it was our turn. Roy stood back with his carbine while the sergeant climbed down and then Vivian. The bearskin dragged heavily when I was hanging by just my hands, and I wished I'd thought to toss it down ahead of me; but then I found a foothold on the cliff and the rest wasn't much more difficult than climbing down a ladder. I jumped the last three feet and grabbed the twisted trunk of a small jackpine to find my balance on the slope.

Roy had no sling on his carbine and so passed it down by its barrel for Yeller to take hold of the stock. I saw then where someone had carved a series of shallow nicks in the walnut near the buttplate. Just five notches seemed low, given the gang's run; but then he might have lost interest since he'd cut the last one.

He was older than any of the others and probably had rheumatism, which the cold would only have aggravated. It took him the best part of five minutes just to climb over the edge, where he rested with one knee braced against it before trusting his weight to the rope. Silhouetted against the slightly lighter sky, he appeared to be shaking. Whitelaw had to bark his name before he decided to push off and hang by his hands, and then his grip wasn't up to it.

He made a croaking little gasp and dropped ten feet. One leg turned under when he hit. I heard the bone snap clean as the rest of him flopped into a heap at Whitelaw's feet.

"My leg's busted! Oh, Mother of God!" His voice cracked.

"Try getting up," Whitelaw said. "Maybe you just banged it good."

Laban stuck out his hand. Roy grasped it and tried to stand. He howled and fell back. Yeller, who had carried the lantern down, held it while the big man leaned over Roy. Laban straightened. "Bone's sticking right out through his pants."

"Jesus God!" Roy groaned. "Oh, Jesus."

Yeller said, "We can't carry him."

"He knows where we're headed," Whitelaw said. "No shots."

Yeller handed the lantern to Laban and got out his skinning knife. Roy was hurting too much to see what was coming until just before Yeller cut his throat. His cry ended in a gurgle.

"Old Roy." Stote stroked his nascent beard. "I'll miss his lies about riding with Frank and Jesse."

Bliss said, "Don't you boys go getting no ideas about me. I can move just as fast with both arms busted."

"Hell, Lolo." Yeller wiped off his knife on Roy's shirt and returned it to its sheath. "You ride with *both* arms stuck out like that, you'll just take off and fly like a big old kite."

"Just don't you boys go getting no ideas about me."

Whitelaw picked up Roy's Springfield from where Yeller had left it leaning against a rock and handed it to the wolf-eyed man. "Keep an eye on Murdock and the redbirds. Hands high, the three of you." He gave Stote the Henry and lifted his own hands. He was playing the part of a prisoner; the only difference was he had one of the confiscated side arms in his belt holster with the flap undone.

With Whitelaw leading we picked our way down the rockfall. It was treacherous going in the dark without the use of our hands. The sergeant, walking in front of me and behind Vivian, put his foot wrong once and would have fallen against the inspector and knocked him down if I hadn't caught him by the shoulders. For my trouble I got a poke in the kidneys from the carbine in the hands of the wolf-eyed man, who thought I'd tried to make a break.

The closer we got to the ground, the

better we could see. The surface of the snow gathered the high dim dusting of starlight and threw it back magnified, like the crystal in a chandelier, slicing the shadows off crisp at the edges and washing everything else in icy white. Even distant details seemed more sharply defined than in daytime, as if I were looking at them through a pinhole in a sheet of foolscap. When we got to within a hundred yards of where the horses were tethered, stamping and shaking their manes for warmth in the silvery smoke of their spent breath, I could make out the snake-shaped blaze on the mustang's forehead. The chestnut coats of the animals belonging to the North-West Mounted gleamed like silk hats.

The mustang spotted us first. Hungry and cold, it raised its head and cut loose with a shrill, querulous neigh.

That was when the night blew apart with orange and blue muzzle-flashes and the *tchocketa-tchocketa-tchock* of the Gatling coughing up its lungful of lead.

28

Charlie Whitelaw went down hard, rolling the rest of the way down the grade and coming out on the level, flat on his stomach, where he lay unmoving while the bullets buzzed over him. I couldn't tell if he was hit or had acted from reflex because I was down myself by that time, knocked flat by the weight of the Mountie sergeant. I didn't know where he was struck or how badly. I shoved him off me and crawled over to where Inspector Vivian lay hugging the pile of rocks that curved down from where the stronghold had begun its collapse one or ten thousand years before. His whole body jerked when I gripped his shoulder; he wasn't dead.

"Is this how you obey orders up here?" I asked him. "Whitelaw made you call down to hold their fire."

I saw one pale eye and the flesh of a bitten-off British smile.

"I could have given them the rest of the month off from up there and they'd not have budged. Ottawa issued a standing order when the police were commissioned, and no one's disobeyed it yet: No bargains. No negotiations. No hostages."

"Not even their own?"

"Especially not their own. No part of the force is more important than the force. The force is not more important than the law. How is the sergeant?"

"Dead or wounded. I can't tell."

"Stupid blighter. No etiquette at all. I never commanded a better man." He made a noise of discomfort.

"Are you hit?"

"Right in the old breadbasket. Good job I haven't had a bite since breakfast. Not that even Saint bloody Bartholomew could do a thing for me out here."

I felt empty. I didn't know why. I didn't like the man.

The deep barking cough of the Gatling had continued, the blue flashes tinged with orange sparking clockwise in a circle and sweeping left and right as the gun turned on its swivel. Ragged small-arms fire opened up, throwing up little arcs of snow from the ground behind a figure running in a crouch across the flat toward the horses, one arm stuck awkwardly out to the side.

Vivian spotted him at the same time I did. "That rotter Bliss! After him, man! Hurry!"

The Gatling had swung right to chop at a number of gang members fleeing in that direction. I pushed myself up and ran, pausing when I reached level ground only to look down at Whitelaw. The back of his coat was stained dark, with blood bubbling out of a hole in the center of the patch. He'd been shot through a lung. When I resumed running the Gatling swiveled back around; I felt the vibration made by the heavy slugs striking the ground behind me. A clump of snow and mud struck my pantslegs. I picked up my pace. If I slipped and fell they'd have to shovel me into the ground.

Bliss had got hold of one of the Mountie horses and hauled himself one-handed into the saddle. He lunged straight at me to run me down. I sidestepped left, putting him and the animal between me and the big gun, and snatched at the bridle. Stinging heat lashed the right side of my face; he'd quirted me with the ends of the reins. I fell backwards, my legs sliding in front of the chestnut's hooves. It reared and a bullet from the Gatling buzzed under its belly and tore the badger hat off my head. The horse leapt over me, scrabbled for its balance in the snow, and took off at the gallop.

I threw myself into a roll, came up alongside the mustang, and got hold of its reins as it was straining to rear against the tether. I fumbled for the loop, slipped it, and got a foot into the stirrup just as it took off. I groped for the saddle horn and hung on in a crouch Comanche-style, using the horse for a shield. Something thudded into the mustang's side, it grunted and stumbled as if the wind had been knocked out of it, but caught its balance and found its pace; a slug must have struck the saddle.

The Gatling continued to chatter, with lighter rounds cracking and popping in between, but by then we were moving too fast to make a good target in the ghostly light conditions. I got my other leg over the horse's back and bent low for speed. Bliss's chestnut had left a clear trail in the snow, with here and there a spot the size of a silver dollar that looked black on the white surface. One or both had been hit, although I couldn't tell how badly.

Mountie animals were bred for speed, but cow ponies are accustomed to cutting through scrub and cactus and are tough to beat on the flat. I knew I was gaining on him when something cracked overhead and I realized it was a ball from my own Deane-Adams. It didn't slow me down. The odds of hitting anything with a belt gun from horseback are too small to figure, and with his left arm out of action Bliss couldn't neglect the reins long enough to take aim. I hunched lower and raked the mustang's flanks with my spurs. The sound of gunfire faded behind us like something belonging to someone else's battle.

We kept it up for what felt like hours. Most likely it was no more than ten minutes before we entered some rolling country north of the lake, and I slacked off a little in case he'd decided to dismount and set up an ambush from a crease between hills. As I swung down, a bullet split the air where my head had been a second earlier, followed by the report.

I saw the fading phosphorescence of the muzzle flare, squeaked the Evans from the scabbard on my side of the horse, and snapped off a shot in that direction to keep him busy while I got into position for a better shot. I sank to one knee in the snow, wrapped the reins loosely around my boot to discourage the mustang from bolting, and drew a bead just above a dark oblong that lay across Bliss's trail some four hundred feet ahead. I guessed what it was without wasting time looking any harder; either the chestnut had been wounded and had given out finally, or Bliss had killed it to make a breastwork.

I was still lining up the sights when flame spurted again. He was using the rifle that had come with the horse, but he was unfamiliar with it or he was a lot less handy with a long gun than he was with his bowie because I never found out where the bullet went. I fired at the spot, jacked in a fresh round, and followed it up.

There was a long silence then. I unwound the reins from my ankle, looped them around each of the mustang's forelegs in a makeshift hobble, and moved away from it in a duckwalk. Just then a volley broke out from near the carcass up the trail — he was racking them in as fast as he could squeeze the trigger — and I threw myself flat on my belly to wait it out.

When it stopped I came up again, just in time to see something dark moving quickly against the snow beyond the carcass. Bliss was making a run. I took careful aim, leading the moving thing slightly with the barrel, but he changed courses abruptly just as I squeezed off, and I wasted the next shot jerking to adjust. I lost him then.

I let a minute go by I couldn't afford, in case he was playing possum and waiting for me to show myself. Then I went back to the mustang and slipped its hobble.

I led the horse to the spot where the chestnut had gone down. It lay on its side with its tongue out and its eyes grown satiny soft, a great gout of blood glittering on its exposed side. The bullet had passed through both its lungs and exited there, and being a horse the animal hadn't thought to fall down until it was strangling in its own blood.

My Deane-Adams lay in the snow near where Bliss had knelt to use the Mountie rifle. I brushed it off, checked the load, replaced the spent shells with cartridges from my belt, and reunited it with its holster. Then I got back aboard the mustang and kneed it into the path of footprints in the snow. I kept it to a walk to avoid galloping into another ambush.

The moon and I came over the next hill at the same time. Now the white landscape was as bright as the desert by daylight. The trail of footprints made a straight black line over the hill beyond. Beyond *that* was black sky stained by uneven light: the glow of a large campfire.

Most fugitives in Bliss's position, pursued and finding themselves approaching other men, would have changed their course in the direction of friendly darkness. From the beginning, Lorenzo Bliss and Charlie Whitelaw had not behaved like any other pair of outlaws. Hunted, they had never stopped hunting. Fire meant people. People were game, a source of supplies and weapons and fresh horses, soft and secure in their numbers and easily disposed of by a man on the prod. The trail divided the hill in a straight line toward the light.

Nearing the top of that hill I stepped down and led the mustang. I added a hundred yards to my journey circling around to the west to keep the moon from silhouetting me from behind.

"You will lay the rifle at your feet."

The owner of the voice had followed my plan as carefully as I had. He stood facing me on the downslope of the hill, just as if he were blocking an existing road instead of a mound of undisturbed snow.

I didn't recognize the voice at first. Too much had happened since I had heard it last. But the mackinaw the man wore looked familiar, the white man's garment making a strong contrast with the braided silver of his long hair and the dusky face that looked as if it had been hacked out of red sandstone. And I had seen the watch chain before, glittering now like a thread of molten silver in the moonlight.

"We've met before," I said. "I didn't know your name then. You are Piapot, chief of the great Cree Nation."

Some Indians were mollified when a white man remembered to address them with the respect they took for granted when it was one of their own speaking. This one just told me again to lay my rifle at my feet. His tone was without threat or anger, but indicated clearly that he would not repeat himself a second time. I obeyed, moving slowly. He stood with his hands loose at his sides without a weapon showing, but there were others standing behind him, vague shadows against the flicker of the fire burning at the base of the hill. I'd been under the gun too many times not to recognize the feeling.

"You are the man who would not give us one of your rifles."

That impressed more than it frightened. The incident had taken place weeks ago and four hundred miles to the south. He had to have seen many white men in the time between, and we all look alike to many Indians. I didn't even consider denying it. "Yes," I said, and took a chance. "And you are the man whose medicine healed me after I was shot on the Saskatchewan."

He was silent long enough for me to wonder if I'd been mistaken about that after all.

"The medicine was not mine," he said. "Small Man is our shaman. It is against your law to kill another white skin, though it does not stop you from doing it. Your death would have brought harm to the crazy woman who shot you, and she is good medicine to the Cree. Therefore you did not die."

"I brought food to the crazy woman. She thought I was there to harm her. She made me well. I am not angry."

"You said before you had business." He buzzed the word with which he was only half familiar. "Is that the reason you have come all this way?"

"Yes. I'm a deputy United States marshal from the territory of Montana. I am hunting the men who killed the crazy woman's family and friends and made her crazy. I mean to bring them home to hang."

"You were chasing the man whose arm is broken."

"Yes. His trail led me here."

"You cannot have him. He will answer to the Cree."

"Answer for what? All his crimes are against the whites."

Piapot put a hand in one of the mackinaw's side pockets and drew something out of it. As he stretched it between his hands my stomach did a slow turn and landed with a thud.

"He had this on him. It is not the scalp of a white man or woman."

"It isn't," I said. "He cut it off the body of Wolf Shirt, a Sioux chief."

A brief pause was all he gave up to show surprise. "The man whose arm is broken killed Wolf Shirt?"

"No. He died of disease. The man with the broken arm is named Bliss. He took the scalp as a souvenir."

"I do not know this word."

"A trophy. He said he always wanted a Sioux scalp. He cut it off Wolf Shirt where he was laid out for burial."

"I do not understand why a man would want to claim a scalp from a man he did not kill. I will never understand why white men do what they do. Yet our friends the

Sioux tell us the whites in America wish the red men to live as they."

"I stop trying to think the way men like Bliss think once I find out where they are," I said. "If you spend too much time in your enemy's skull you become the enemy."

He folded the scalp. No honor guard ever folded Old Glory with more reverence. "It is the — business — of a chief's woman to stay with him until he is buried. What was Wolf Shirt's woman doing when the man Bliss stole his scalp?"

I told him what Yeller had done when the woman tried to stop him from stealing the dead chief's lance to make Bliss's splints. He was as silent as the hills while I told him that Yeller was either dead or in Mountie custody. I hoped I was right.

"Bliss will answer to the Cree," Piapot said again.

Just then I heard a high-pitched curse from somewhere on the other side of the fire. The mix of Spanish and English ended in a ragged whimper I can still hear all these years later.

The chief spoke as if he had not heard it. "I see you still have two rifles. Will you now give us one?"

"No."

One of the men standing behind him seemed to know that English word very well. He said something to the chief with an edge that went up my spine like a rusty blade.

Piapot didn't appear to be listening. He folded the scalp once more, taking more time with it than simple respect alone commanded. Gently he returned it to his pocket.

"This is twice you have entered the land of the Cree and refused to pay tribute."

"I'd stop coming if I could figure out where Canada left off and the land of the Cree began. It seems to be spreading."

"It is not. In my youth it stretched from the Great Sea of Ice to the stinging sands where only the gila and the Apache live. When the snow came we rode down to where it is always warm and when the great heat came we rode up to where the pines grow through the clouds. In all that time we saw nothing of the white man. Now there is only one way we can ride so that we do not see him: North, where the white man will not live. There perhaps we can hunt and fight our old enemies and make love to our women and not hear white men gnawing down the trees like beaver to build the railway to bring more white men. When that happens, there will be nowhere left to go but out on the Great Sea of Ice."

He turned his back on me then and walked down the hill. The others lingered for a moment after he passed them, then followed. I was alone.

After a moment I picked up the Evans and returned it to its scabbard. When I put my foot in the stirrup, something fell out of my pocket. It was the leather pouch containing the bones of an African eagle, a charm to see me home safe. I scooped it up and put it back in my pocket. I still have it.

29

The firing had stopped by the time I got back to the lake, although smoke was still billowing, eye-stinging clouds laden with sulphur and mingling with steam from men and horses. To avoid getting shot I whistled loudly — "My Country, 'Tis of Thee" was the tune I chose, but if they decided to take it for "God Save the Queen," so much the better — riding with my bearskin spread open with the six-pointed star pinned to my shirt for the first time since I was almost shot out from behind it in '76. Even then, I learned later, a Mountie sharpshooter had been sighting in on me with a Martini-Henry when Philippe du la Rochelle put a hand on his arm and bought a gash in his scalp from the butt of Lieutenant Ponsoby's side arm for his trouble. It was only then that someone had spotted the badge.

I was ordered to dismount anyway, disarmed, and compelled to tell my story to the lieutenant before I was taken to a tent where Inspector Urban Vivian lay on a bedroll with his shirt off, and a Mountie wearing a bloody apron in place of his tunic was tying off his bandages. A trooper was pounding home the last stake into the frozen ground when Vivian glared at me in the light of a hissing lantern. His face was the color of water beneath his sunburn, his eyes unnaturally large and swimming. I knew the look of a corpse in the making, but I gave him the details anyway, knowing I'd have to do it all over again for whoever took his place. He was too weak to ask questions, but I could feel his irritation at my unsatisfactory report. The lieutenant made it clear that I was confined to camp until such time as my story could be passed on to Ottawa and instructions came back.

Vivian died just before dawn. He had served with distinction in Abyssinia and at Roarke's Drift, holding out in the latter place with a handful of British regulars against the same 40,000 Zulu warriors who had destroyed the Queen's army only a few days before at Isandhlwana. His body was packed with salt and shipped back to England for burial with full military honors, the first in a family of candle-makers and cloth merchants to receive them.

Corporal Gale Barrymore, whose mother had died during the ocean voyage to the New World and whose father lived on a government pension in Ottawa, was laid to rest in that city.

I understand the names of the Mounties who were killed at the stronghold are engraved among others on a brass plaque mounted on a marble wall in the capitol building in Ottawa. I don't know if the official record states that Inspector Urban Vivian was slain by his own men, but I approve of the honor. He led thirteen enemies of the Crown straight into police fire, knowing that it meant his own death. I admired him. I just couldn't get along with him.

The sergeant major's name was Rice. Although the bullet that smashed his pelvis gave him a permanent limp, he was promoted to inspector in 1891 for his part in a forty-seven-day manhunt resulting in the arrest and conviction of a Canadian Army deserter named Oberlin for the ambush-murder of three wealthy excursionists on the Yukon Trail. A year later he was considered for the office of superintendent, but rejected for his extreme views on the subject of criminal punishment, notably the suggestion to revive the medieval practice of drawing and quartering. He retired soon after.

Four members of the Bliss-Whitelaw Gang were killed in the opening fire at Cree Lake, including young Stote, the Negro Redfoot, and the wolf-eyed man, a quarter-breed Ute named Dick Night-hunter. The fourth was not Yeller, born Gunther Braun in Pennsylvania; he was captured along with Laban and three others, tried in Ottawa, and hanged for the murder of a Métis family of four and a Roman Catholic priest named Capet on Lake Athabasca. The big Negro and one other were condemned, as well. The remaining pair were sentenced to a lifetime at hard labor in the penitentiary at Quebec.

Two more who had been with Bliss and Whitelaw at the stronghold slipped away during the fight; their footprints were traced to a half-moon-shaped cleft hol-lowed out by glaciers a mile east of the lake, where a number of horses had been picketed. The man who had been watching the animals was never found, but a month later a farmer named Donalbain shot to death two men he caught stealing horses from his barn below the border in Mon-tana. Pinkerton detectives came out from

Fort Benton to take pictures of the corpses and make Bertillon measurements, then sent the results to the home office in Chicago, where the two were identified from penitentiary records as Virgil Hearn and John Thomson, both of whom had served time in the territories for armed robbery. Thomson's brother Ned was the fourth man killed by the Mounties at the stronghold, and so that loose end was considered tied down for good and all.

I never saw Philippe or his family after we parted company at the Mountie camp. I found the little Métis sitting on King Henry's wooden saddle on the ground near a little campfire, not far from where the prisoners were being held under guard, complaining in mixed French and English that Fleurette was tying the bandage too tight around his scalp wound. He wouldn't say how it happened, and Fleurette hadn't the English for it, but Claude broke his silence for the second time since we'd started out, providing a full and lucid account of how his father had managed to keep my name off a brass plaque in Ottawa; or more likely a wooden cross in Helena. (His choice of words and phrases puzzled me until years later, when I read *Wuthering Heights* for the first time.)

Philippe barked at him. The boy stuck out his lip. Then his father said something just as gruff, but not as harsh, tweaked Claude's already scarlet cheek hard enough to hurt, and sent him off with a smack on the rump to look for his book and a spot by the fire.

"That was taking a chance," I said. "Once the killing starts, it's hard to stop, no matter what kind of training you've had."

He showed his gold teeth. "I have earned those double eagles, yes?"

I fished them out of the sack. When he reached for them, I dropped them into his palm and laid the Evans rifle across his lap with my other hand.

He looked up. "You will come home with us and I will give you the buffalo robe."

"I won't need it. After Canada, winter in Montana will feel like springtime in Missouri."

"That was not our bargain." He pocketed the coins and held out the rifle for me to take. I didn't.

Fleurette said something quietly. After a moment he said, *"Bon,"* and returned the rifle to his lap. *"Merci, monsieur le depute.* Deputy Marshal Murdock."

"Page will do. It's easier to say." I went back into my pocket. "Good luck finding ammunition. These are as many shells as I could gather up." I tipped the handful of brass empties into his hand. He gripped mine before letting go.

"The Métis are not without ingenuity in these things," he said. "You will return for the trial, no?"

I glanced toward the tent where the man who had dressed Vivian's wound was working on Whitelaw. "My part ends here. Anyway, I doubt he'll live long enough to see a courtroom."

"He will recover. A man with so much poison in him does not die like other men."

They had eaten, but there was some rabbit left and Fleurette insisted on warming it over the fire even though I was hungry enough to eat it cold, or for that matter with the fur on. We said good night and I cleared a space nearby for my bedroll and went to sleep immediately. When I awoke at dawn, the family had pulled out for home.

Three years later, the Métis rebel leader Louis Riel Jr. returned from exile to lead a second insurrection against British rule in Canada. The civil war came to a head in

May 1885 in the village of Batoche, where two hundred Métis held out for four days against nearly a thousand militiamen and Canadian regulars before they were overrun. During the standoff, Métis sharpshooters supplemented their waning ammunition with pebbles, nails, and metal buttons against some seventy-thousand Gatling rounds and hammering blows from seven-pounders. I did not hear if Philippe Louis-Napoleon Charlemagne Voltaire Murat du la Rochelle and his marvelous Evans rifle were among the sharpshooters, or if he was one of those tried in Regina for treason and sentenced to life at hard labor, but I remembered what he had told me about Métis ingenuity. Riel himself was convicted in Regina of treason and incitement to rebellion and hanged.

At about the same time, eight members of the Cree Nation were hanged in Regina for their part in an attack on the Mountie stockade at Battleford in conjunction with Métis rebels. Chief Piapot was not among them, having died of natural causes the year before near the Arctic Circle, the place the Cree called the Great Sea of Ice. Construction on the Canadian Pacific Railway resumed and sped to completion.

The free African community of

Shulamite barely survived the century. In the nineties the generation that had grown up since slavery went to the cities to look for work. Their children joined the Canadian colored regiments during the World War, and when they returned they did not go back to the settlement except only briefly, to visit elderly relatives who spoke of nothing but life on the plantation and the adventure of the Underground Railroad. By then developers had bought and torn down the cabins and the great lodge, replaced them with proper houses, and renamed the place in favor of something less contentious. Its current residents have never heard of Brother Hebron or Queen Fidelity. The leading church is Southern Baptist.

Nothing was heard of Lorenzo Bliss after the night of the Mountie assault on the Sioux stronghold at Cree Lake, although the legend grew up that he had somehow escaped Indian justice to rob Canadian trains with Bill Miner's gang in 1906. They say Jesse James and Billy the Kid were never killed either. I suppose somewhere there's a private club where these latter-day Lazaruses gather to drink and play cards and compare stories of life on the scout.

Charlie Whitelaw, the renegade Cherokee who with Lorenzo Bliss led a band of murderers on a bloody rampage from the Nations to the wilderness of Canada, beat all the odds and recovered from his injuries. After six months he was declared medically fit to stand trial, but the proceedings were delayed for another year while the U.S. State Department and the Canadian Ministry of Justice fought over who got first crack at him. Finally, in response to a letter from President Arthur, Sir John Macdonald, the prime minister, agreed to remand the prisoner over to the American authorities once a verdict had been reached in Ottawa. He was quickly found guilty on twenty-three counts of armed robbery, rape, arson, and murder, and sentenced to death, whereupon he was transported under guard to Helena. There Judge Blackthorne ordered him to hang following his conviction on thirty-eight counts of capital crime in territories belonging to the United States.

As it turned out, though, he didn't hang even once.

In June 1883, while awaiting execution in the Montana territorial penitentiary at Deer Lodge, Whitelaw strangled to death a guard who passed too near his cell and used the guard's key to unlock the door. He got almost to the end of the cellblock before Halloran, the captain of the guard, stuck a sawed-off ten-gauge shotgun between the bars of the block door and blew him to pieces at a range of three feet. What was left of him was shoveled into the ground in the prison courtyard without so much as a plain wooden cross to mark the spot. He was twenty-four years old.

They say you always remember where you were when you heard such news: I suppose I'm the exception. All I know for sure is I wasn't in a room that contained a billiard table.

The employees of Thorndike Press hope you have enjoyed this Large Print book. All our Large Print titles are designed for easy reading, and all our books are made to last. Other Thorndike Press Large Print books are available at your library, through selected bookstores, or directly from the publisher.

For more information about titles, please call:

(800) 223-1244
(800) 223-6121

To share your comments, please write:

Publisher
Thorndike Press
295 Kennedy Memorial Drive
Waterville, ME 04901